GROWING UP WITH B.G.

Don Hancock

To: Joyce
Thanks for
everything!
Enjoy!

Don

Growing Up With B.G.

© 2007

Don Hancock

ISBN: 978-0-9795258-9-6

Warwick House Publishers
720 Court Street
Lynchburg, VA 24504

DEDICATION

This book is dedicated to a special group of people who have always loved to laugh and enjoy life: my family. Humor has enabled us to get through some very difficult times, while making the good times richer and more enjoyable. Within that family, I am especially honored to dedicate this book to my younger brother Ron ("B.G."). He is a Christian brother as well as my biological brother, and one of the best friends I've ever known. I love you, Bro!

Ron and Don, 1985

IN MEMORY

I wrote this book with constant thoughts of those dear family members who have passed away. My mother, Geneva Ruth (Dotson) Hancock, and father, Charles Isaac Hancock, will never be forgotten. Dad always enjoyed a good laugh! Sharon Eich Hancock was my sister-in-law and appreciated my jokes. She would have loved this book! And my precious daughter, Kelly Ruth Hancock, was funny and vivacious with a zest for life and a great sense of humor. I love you all and miss you every day!

"There is a time for everything...
a time to weep and a time to laugh."
(Ecclesiastes 3)

THANK YOU

Thanks to my family members for their patience and encouragement. Ron reviewed the manuscript and offered suggestions while agreeing to let me "skewer" him. My daughter, Jennifer, also reviewed some of the manuscript (right before "rolling her eyes" and muttering, "Heaven help us!"). My wife, Robin, allowed me to realize my dream of writing this book. Her editing expertise and computer assistance were invaluable. I'll be taking her out to dinner and giving her back-rubs for a *long* time! A dear friend, Stue Glaser, urged me to continue after he read some of the book. Darrell Laurant of the *Lynchburg News and Advance* provided advice and encouragement, as did Joyce Maddox at Warwick House Publishing. The book would never have been completed without Joyce's patient assistance.

My sincere thanks to all of you!

ABOUT THE AUTHOR

Don Hancock lives in beautiful Bedford County, Virginia, with his wife, Robin. They have been married for thirty-five years. Their daughter, Jennifer, lives in North Carolina. Don has a B.S. in Psychology from Frostburg State University in Maryland and a M.A. in Counseling from Liberty University in Virginia. He enjoys reading, hiking, fishing, carpentry, and writing.

CONTENTS

INTRODUCTION

It is impossible for anyone to imagine the pain and suffering inflicted on the siblings of a brilliant child. Sometimes the brilliant one is younger than his or her siblings and this only exacerbates the problem. This was certainly my experience during childhood as my younger brother, Ron, continually surpassed me due to his amazing intellect. My meager accomplishments were repeatedly eclipsed by him as he humiliated and embarrassed me time after time.

My parents were not very helpful as I tried to deal with this situation. Mom and Dad were unable to understand why I continually lagged behind a brother who was thirteen months younger, and they were less than sympathetic at times. I'm sure that they loved me even though I was usually referred to as "Ronald's goofy older brother" or "the slow one" or "what's his name."

I finally sought therapy later in life to help me cope with my difficult childhood. This was short-lived, however, since the therapist (at the end of the first session) asked me to get Ron's autograph for her. She also asked me, "Is he seeing anyone?" I finally went ballistic when she said, "Now, what was your name again?" in preparation for scheduling the next session. She mentioned something about "displaced aggression" as the security guards pulled me off of her and forcefully escorted me from the office. I decided that the best therapy would be to write this story.

So "buckle up" because this story will be one wild ride. If you've ever "been there" in a similar situation with a Super Sibling, then a lot of this will sound familiar to you. Perhaps you'll say to yourself, "That guy really knows what he's talking about!" Some who read this have never been in such dire straits but have wondered what it was like for the rest of us. They never shared a bedroom with an obnoxious over-achieving brother or sister who deserved to be smothered with a pillow. Read this and you'll gain understanding (and sympathy) for those of us who were persecuted in childhood by our brilliant siblings as we stood in their shadows.

This story will introduce the reader to some interesting and oddball characters and events. You will, at times, wonder if some of the story really happened. I can assure you that all persons and events are portrayed accurately and without prejudice or embellishment. I began to formulate this story during my time at Woodstock and know that it's the result of clear thinking and totally accurate recall.* It not only reveals how my brother bested me time and again but also recounts the zany antics of a bunch of wacky kids. Return with me to those thrilling days of yesteryear: no Internet, no MTV…just kids with lots of imagination and a knack for creating chaos.

Welcome to *Growing Up With B.G.*, the story of my childhood with my brother, Ron, and our friends. Ron will henceforth be referred to as B.G. because he was the "Boy Genius." I no longer refer to him as B.G. now that I'm older and wiser but instead call him M. B. F. (My Best Friend).

* OK, let me be honest. It's *fiction!* This book *may* contain some factual, historical and chronological inaccuracies when referring to specific people, places and events. Get over it!

THE EARLY YEARS

B.G. arrived on the scene when I was thirteen months old and I didn't like him from the beginning. He was too cute (at least, that's what everyone said) and he cried a lot. Everyone who came to our house had to hold him, rock him, and make lots of ridiculous baby-talk noises to him. This only got worse as time went on and I quickly got tired of B.G. being the center of attention. No one even knew he was going to be the Boy Genius at that time because he could not talk. He must have been the *Baby* Genius because B.G. had everyone wrapped around his chubby little fingers.

As the months passed by, I noticed that B.G. had no job or marketable skills. He got away with sleeping most of the day and soiling his diaper while I had to be a "big boy" and poop in the potty. This became my main task for quite some time and probably helped to qualify me for later employment. I worked for the federal government during part of my adult years, sitting on my butt and producing a lot of stuff that deserved to be flushed.

B.G. also had the advantage when it came to meals. He was able to secure his nourishment right from the breast while I had to be a "big boy" and drink from a bottle. This never made sense to me since there were *two* fountains and B.G. could only drink from one at a time. B.G. was never big on sharing, however, and he became quite upset when I approached the idle breast. I was looking for the "La Leche Express Lane" only to have B.G. proclaim, "This aisle closed!" This deprivation early in life profoundly affected me and probably explains my fascination with "Victoria's Secret" catalogues. (My wife has never bought into this theory.)

The months and years passed by and B.G. became a thorn in my side. He followed me everywhere since he started walking at six months of age! That was bad enough, but then I had to cope with him starting to talk when he was only one! He was speaking in complete sentences by the time he was fifteen months old, correcting my grammar at eighteen months, and conversing fluently in English, Spanish, French, and German at age two! This brat wore out his welcome with me real fast!

It was obvious to all that my brother was something special. It was also obvious that I was not! Everyone wanted to see what he would do once he started school since the kid appeared to be some kind of Junior Einstein. My troubles had only begun.

"Best Friends"
Ron "B.G." (left) and Don (right)

SCHOOL DAZE IN BALTIMORE

B.G. started school and quickly left the rest of us kids in the dust. He was only in the first grade for *five* weeks! The kid was so smart that he amazed and astounded everyone. He was taken upstairs to one of the sixth grade classrooms so that the students there could listen to him read. The kids, teachers, and principal were in awe of B.G. and his fame quickly spread throughout Hawthorne Elementary School.

The next thing that I knew, Mr. Know-it-All shows up in second grade! I couldn't believe it because that was *my* domain and I had worked hard to get there. I had to put in a full year of first grade to get promoted to second grade but B.G. got a "cakewalk" after five measly weeks. What a raw deal! Was there no justice? I had gone along with the program and done everything that the first grade teacher asked of me. I colored inside the lines, raised my hand before talking, and held it when I had to pee before the bathroom break. And what did all that accomplish?

Don in first grade (1956)

B.G. was really starting to get under my skin. Second grade was not the place for some smart-aleck six-year-old who failed to "pay his dues" in first grade just because he was some kind of Brainiac. I firmly believed that you had to "do the time" in first grade before you could move up to the big leagues. I started talking to my friend, Dominic, about all of this. Dominic said that he had "connections" and could arrange for my brother to "just disappear one day." Dominic offered to take care of this for me if I would give him my Roy Rogers lunch box. I was fond of that lunch box and cared a lot more for it than for B.G. I certainly wanted to bid farewell to B.G., but I could not bring myself to part with that lunch box. It had Roy Rogers and Dale Evans on the front with Roy's horse, Trigger, and the wonder dog, Bullet, on the back. So I declined Dominic's offer and he was *not* happy at all, reminding me that *I* could "just disappear one day."

Dominic had a mean streak. He was a seven-year-old to be reckoned with and not someone that you wanted as your enemy. I bought him a lot of ice cream bars when the Good Humor ice cream truck visited our neighborhood. One day the Good Humor man came by in his truck with the bells ringing and all of the neighborhood kids in tow. When I tried to purchase Dominic's Good Humor bar, the ice cream man said he was all out. Dominic was not happy and told the Good Humor man that he could "just disappear one day." I think Dominic later ate ice cream while incarcerated in a Maryland correctional facility, but that's another story.

THE WONDER CHILD

My brother, despite his amazing intellect, seemed to lack discernment in his dealings with other kids. He had a unique way of getting under their skin and making them angry. I often thought that if he was really such a genius then he should have known when to keep his mouth shut. But no, not the Wonder Child! B.G. was always correcting the grammar of the other kids, reminding them of the rules during ball games, and generally annoying the heck out of them.

B.G. got beat up a lot as a result of his big mouth and I frankly enjoyed this a great deal. I got to watch Mr. Smartie Pants get just what he deserved without hurting my fist on his hard head and getting into trouble with Mom and Dad.

Dad finally took me aside one day and told me that I needed to look out for B.G. and take care of him because I was

On our front sidewalk (B.G. on left, Don on right).
Note how close the school was (upper left).

7

his big brother and "that's what big brothers do." Dad knew that B.G. was a pain in the butt to me and the other kids and deserved to get punched out. Dad had a vested interest in B.G. remaining healthy, however, since the kid was only six but a-dept at balancing Dad's checkbook and tuning up the car. I got tired of fighting to protect B.G. so I told him to stop shooting off his mouth. (Right! Like that was going to happen!) This was futile so I saved up my allowance, went to the hardware store, and bought a roll of duct tape. I got a little carried away one day and didn't stop with just taping B.G.'s *mouth* shut. He caused quite a stir later that day as he stumbled through our neighborhood completely wrapped up in duct tape. The police came out later, interviewed our hysterical elderly neighbor, and searched in vain for that "little silver mummy." Mom and Dad grounded me for two weeks for that little stunt, but Dominic and the other kids were quite supportive.

B.G. was bright...no doubt about it. I mean, how many six-year-olds can tune up a car? He not only tuned it up—he improved it! We were the first family in Baltimore to own a car with electronic ignition. In 1957! B.G. was amazing! He was always creating and inventing, improving and "tweaking." He once took a Swiss Army knife, some duct tape, and the "rabbit ears" antenna off of our old Philco black and white T.V. and intercepted secret radio transmissions from the Aberdeen Proving Ground. Another time he picked up President Eisenhower singing in the shower at the White House! B.G. once took my Tinker Toys and Lincoln Logs and built a model of the space shuttle. In 1957!

B.G. was truly a boy genius and the mind behind most of our modern technological marvels. Dominic and I were ready to beat him up one day because we caught him messing around with our "phone" (two tin cans connected by a string). We were amazed as B.G. programmed each can to receive either analog or digital signals. Everything was fine until he started explaining the difference between analog and digital. We were so annoyed that we beat him up anyway and then went off in search of some more duct tape. That kid just needed an attitude adjustment!

REVENGE IS SWEET

B.G. continued to amaze people as the years went by. His abilities to create and invent were unsurpassed by even the top scientists of the day. I, of course, seemed more and more inferior to B.G. as he excelled in Quantum Physics (in third grade) and other subjects which I can't even spell.

B.G. seemed to have the creative juices really flowing on Saturday mornings. Mom and Dad would sleep in while B.G. was up at the crack of dawn. All I wanted to do was sleep late and then watch cartoons. I had just started to watch *Heckle and Jeckle* one Saturday morning (while eating a bowl of Fruit Loops) when along came little Mr. Know-it-All to inform me that H&J were "magpies and not crows." Now, to say I'm *not* a "morning person" would be an understatement. You just do *not* want to mess with me early in the morning. B.G. was apparently unable or unwilling to grasp this truth so he proceeded to lecture me about avian science. He did not realize that if I said Heckle and Jeckle were crows, then that was it! Case closed! End of discussion! Arguing with me about it (while standing in front of the TV blocking my view) was a sure way to end up with a nose full of Fruit Loops.

B.G., despite all his brilliance, was really pretty stupid at times. This was one of those times. He was determined to learn "the hard way" on this particular Saturday as he went on and on with his annoying lecture. Bad move! He ended up picking Fruit Loops out of his nostrils (and then proceeded to eat them!) all through *Fury*, *My Friend Flicka*, and *Sky King*. He finally removed the last one about the time that Johnny Quest found his lost dog, Bandit, in the clutches of an evil mummy on the Island of Doom.

It seemed wise to B.G. at this point to leave me alone and go off to create something that would make the world safer for mankind. (How about a nose guard to keep out Fruit Loops, Wonder Boy?) He proceeded to create and install a miniature video camera in my Robert the Robot, along with a remote control device. B.G. (the world's greatest tattle-tale) planned to use his invention to monitor my activities and then report back to Mom and Dad. Well, there was a problem. B.G. sent the robot into Mom and Dad's room by mistake and ended up monitoring something else! Mom and Dad were surprised, to say the least, and Dad drop-kicked old Roberto right out of the bedroom window!

Dad knew that the robot was *my* toy, so guess who got blamed? I was in some deep trouble. Mom and Dad later discussed the situation and decided on two things: (1) There was no way that *I* could have programmed the robot to film Mom and Dad "wrestling." I just didn't have the brains to do it (sometimes it pays to be a "D minus" student). They concluded that it had to be the work of an evil genius, and only B.G. had the qualifications. So I was "off the hook" and B.G. got punished for a change (finally!). (2) It was time for Dad to have "The Talk" with B.G. and me since we were obviously curious about sex (B.G. maybe; I just wanted to watch cartoons).

Anyway, "The Talk" was postponed for some time (more about that in a later chapter), but B.G.'s punishment was immediate. He was grounded for two weeks and had to pay me for the permanently damaged robot. The following Saturday I sat on the couch eating Captain Crunch cereal and drinking Ovaltine. *Howdy Doody* was on TV and B.G. was confined to his room. I heard some noise from Mom and Dad's room and figured that they were "wrestling" again. Yeah, it was a good day for everyone but B.G.!

TOP SECRET

B.G. rarely got caught or punished due to his misdeeds. He possessed a unique ability to implicate *me* in just about everything he did, and time and again he was the champ and I was the chump. I could never figure out if he was truly that clever or if I was just such an easy mark for a manipulative master like B.G.

On those rare occasions when B.G. actually *did* get caught and punished, I was ecstatic! Just to see Brainiac get taken down a notch or two was sheer joy for me. I delighted in "rubbing his nose in it" and harassing him mercilessly because those times of triumph for me were so rare. I usually went too far, however, and ended up with Mom or Dad asking me, "So, do you want some of that, too?" Then I would find that *I* was in trouble for "making poor little Ronald feel bad." Oh, please! It was like having the referee at a football game throw a penalty flag for "excessive celebration" or "taunting the opposition" just because someone danced in the end zone after scoring a touchdown.

B.G. and I loved to be outdoors running around like a couple of wild animals. Mom and Dad realized this and knew that one of the most effective punishments for us was confinement to our rooms. We *hated* it! This was a punishment guaranteed to get our attention, and it had the desired effect. We usually "shaped up" quickly after a short time in "solitary." There was no such thing as "Time Out" in those days. The only "time out" period was the interlude between the spanking by Mom and the spanking by Dad. We got spanked with anything that the Parental Units could get their hands on—belt, paddle, switch, fly swatter—you name it and we got whacked with it! All you could do was grit your teeth and endure. It helped if you could quickly manufacture some tears, real or fake. B.G. usually managed to slip a Sears catalogue down into the back of his pants to provide some padding. Then he would do the whole weeping and wailing with fake tears like he was about to die. Mom and/or Dad would quickly stop the corporal punishment since B.G. sounded so pitiful, turn to the other and exclaim, "That boy sure has a hard butt!" Give me a break!

My brother didn't enjoy the time in his room but he handled it much better than I did due to his creativity. He was quite adept at amusing himself as he invented, created, and "tweaked." After the "Robot incident" he had to spend two weeks in his room and he put the time to good use.

B.G. got out his Super Deluxe Erector Set and built a fifty-foot tower on the floor in ten-foot sections. He took the five sections out through his bedroom window into the back yard and assembled them into the fifty-foot tower. He climbed back into his bedroom through the window, quietly opened his bedroom door ever so slightly, and checked to see if things were "all clear." Dad was napping on the couch in the living room and Mom and I were at the grocery store. So B.G. sneaked into the kitchen and "borrowed" Mom's big roll of Reynolds Wrap and stopped by my room to "borrow" my Hula Hoop. He then

Don and Ron in 1958

returned to his room, exited via the window, and went back outside to the tower. He covered the Hula Hoop with the aluminum foil and then climbed to the top of the tower while holding the Hula Hoop in his teeth. B.G. proceeded to mount the foil-covered Hula Hoop to the top of the tower and then did some calculations, adjustments, repositioning, and "tweaking." He then climbed down and returned to his room just as Mom and I got back from the A&P Market. It was almost dark so none of us noticed the fifty-foot monstrosity in the back yard. No one (except B.G.) knew anything for quite awhile. I was frustrated because I could not find my Hula Hoop and Mom was upset because she "forgot to put Reynolds Wrap on the grocery list."

That evening one of the neighbors called to ask Dad if he had noticed any interference on the TV. The neighbor was frustrated because *The Ed Sullivan Show* was "fuzzy" but Dad only replied, "I don't watch that show anymore since he had on those long-haired rock and roll singers." Yes, my father hated the Beatles.

The next morning Mom and Dad finally saw the tower in the back yard. They immediately knew that I could not possibly be responsible for such a creation. "Ronald, get in here NOW!" bellowed Dad from the living room. B.G. ran to the living room with me right behind him. I knew that something was wrong just by listening to the tone of Dad's voice, not to mention the *volume*! I was anxious to see B.G. get punished *again* before he had even finished serving his sentence for his previous transgression (the Robot affair). Mom heard Dad yell so she ran to the living room to plead for the life of her baby boy before Dad killed him. I thought to myself, "Man, this is going to be sooo good! C'mon, Pop, take your belt off and flog the little over-achiever within an inch of his life!" But wait, because it was just too good to be true. Before Dad could get a grip on B.G.'s scrawny little neck, the doorbell rang. Dad opened the door and found a couple of four-star generals standing on the front porch! It seems that they had heard about B.G. and his intellectual prowess, as well as his recent fifty-foot creation. I think that we were under constant surveillance to prevent the Russians from kidnapping Wonder Boy, taking him to Moscow, and using his genius for their evil purposes. Anyway, the generals had a hush-hush talk with Mom and Dad in the dining room before handing them a check with a lot of zeroes. Then the generals left and Mom and Dad began to hug and kiss B.G. like crazy! There was also talk about getting a *color* TV and a new Edsel! I could not believe it! Somehow B.G. had come out on top once again. He didn't get punished —he got rewarded! Why? What happened? What was up with those two generals and the big check?

Let me just say that, prior to the Freedom of Information Act, if I told you, I'd have to kill you. Now that many years have passed and all of this has been declassified, I can reveal that B.G.'s tower was used to relay top secret microwave transmissions between Edgewood Arsenal and the Pentagon. This continued for a number of years. No one ever knew about this and it was a well-kept family secret. We just kept telling the neighbors that it was a new-fangled TV antenna as we cashed those government checks and replaced the aluminum foil on the Hula Hoop every month. And when we drove down to the A&P to pick up the Reynolds Wrap, we were traveling in style in a brand new Edsel!

Sometimes life with B.G. was almost tolerable.

THE FACTS OF LIFE—Part One

Speaking of microwaves, B.G. created a microwave oven for my mother in 1958. He told Thelma Lou McGillicuddy next door that I would kiss her if she would give up her Easy Bake Oven. Now Thelma Lou's desire for the taste of my lips was well-known throughout our neighborhood. I mean, the girl had it bad for me! And why not? I couldn't do advanced calculus in my head like Bro Brainiac but I was quite the handsome guy. I was considered a "player" with the ladies in those days, and I was always invited to any "Spin the Bottle" game in the neighborhood. I'd roll into the game with a pack of breath mints in my pocket, ready to pucker up for the lucky ladies and make their day. Heck, I would even bring my own bottle (usually Nehi orange) if necessary.

Thelma Lou found me irresistible, but that was no surprise to me. My hero was Kookie from the TV show *77 Sunset Strip*. He was the guy who invented "cool" and the guy I wanted to be, so I imitated him, and the girls loved it. I wanted to be as cool as Kookie and as brave as the guys on *Rescue 8*. That combination had to be too much for any woman to resist, but I really wished that Thelma Lou had more willpower. She was *not* the girl that *this* eight year-old Romeo wanted to attract.

Thelma Lou was, to put it kindly, not an attractive girl. She had thick glasses *and* braces, along with an annoying habit of passing gas at inappropriate moments. This was the less-than-lovely creature that was in love with me and determined to make me her husband one day. So B.G.'s offer to her was a "no-brainer." She gladly gave up the Easy Bake Oven and my brother "tweaked" it. He invented and installed a magnetron and created the first home microwave oven…in our house in Baltimore…in 1958!

Thelma Lou stopped by one day to collect her "payment" for the oven and I never knew what hit me! See, I knew *noth-*

ing about the deal between B.G. and Thelma Lou. All I knew was that the little Morton's Pot Pies were getting done a lot faster at suppertime. So when Thelma Lou asked me to come out onto the back porch, I didn't suspect a thing. All of a sudden she put the old-fashioned Irish Lip Lock on me and I was overwhelmed, shocked, and embarrassed.

B.G. and some of the guys were up in the tree house and saw the whole thing! They went NUTS! They whistled and hollered like a bunch of idiots while I turned crimson and tried to fight off Thelma Lou (which was not an easy task considering the fever pitch of her passion). Dominic yelled, "Slip her some tongue!" but I had no idea what that was all about. He was a rather precocious young man with a colorful Italian heritage. Dominic seemed to know a lot more about girls than the rest of us (which really wasn't saying a lot). Anyway, Thelma Lou finally let me "come up for air" and she turned toward the tree house and yelled, "THANK YOU!" to my brother. I then realized that this scenario was *his* handiwork and I screamed, "Stay up in that tree house if you want to live, punk!" He hastily pulled up the rope ladder.

Dominic later told me that if things continued to be so sizzling between Thelma Lou and me (yeah, like that was going to happen) then "protection" would be necessary. I had no idea what he was talking about but thought that he wanted to be my bodyguard to keep Thelma Lou away from me (You know… "She could just disappear one day"). Well, Dominic gave me a package of "protection" one day and I opened it up. All I found inside was a balloon (or so I thought) so I blew it up and took it to B.G.'s birthday party. Dad turned three shades of red and asked, "Where did you get that?" B.G. chimed in and said, "Probably out of your top dresser drawer, Dad, and way in the back" just as Mom yelled, "Eat your cake, NOW!" B.G. crammed a huge piece of cake into his mouth with a burning candle still attached. Dad popped the "balloon" and sent me to my room (minus cake). Dominic was rolling on the floor and laughing so hard that he could barely breathe. Dad growled,

"What's so funny, boy?" before giving Dominic a piece of cake and promptly sending him home. All of this excitement was too much for Thelma Lou so she "broke wind" and was also sent home with a piece of cake (so far, I was the only one who misbehaved and still did *not* get any birthday cake).

B.G. (the Birthday Boy) was allowed to eat all the cake that he wanted and he did *not* end up in his room. He was praised by Mom and Dad for inventing the microwave oven, being such a "good boy," and avoiding the antics of his "delinquent" older brother. Mom and Dad *did* remind him to stay out of the dresser drawers in their room, however.

I sat in my room and decided that B.G. was the devil, with Thelma Lou and Dominic obviously under his spell. I longed for a brighter day when well-meaning professionals would intervene in our family and neighborhood, declaring that all of us were dysfunctional and therefore not responsible for our actions. I wished for an opportunity (like the "Jerry Springer Show" years later) which would allow me to tell of my persecution and torment as I punched out B.G. while millions watched on TV.

Don (age 9) and Ron (age 8), Baltimore, Maryland

BOB WHO?

I have to say that B.G. and I had a few good moments. Remember the tree house? B.G. helped me build it during the summer of 1958. I was just going to build your standard tree house…you know…plywood nailed to two by fours nailed onto a tree branch. But that wasn't good enough for B.G., not by a long shot. No, the Wonder Child had to have something a little more elaborate.

B.G. had to design the thing to his exact specifications using detailed blueprints and the latest engineering techniques. He calculated loads, stress factors, the effect of hurricane-force winds on the tree and the tree house, phases of the moon, maximum occupancy…you get the picture. The neighbor's son (who was a senior at M.I.T.) came over to check things out and was totally amazed at B.G.'s work. After B.G. explained it to Mr. M.I.T., the college boy called his professor and received three credits just for spending time at the "B.G. School of Engineering." B.G. was awarded an honorary doctorate!

We ended up with a condo in an oak tree! We had a bathroom, hot and cold running water, cable TV, a pool table, an elevator, a kitchenette, a fireplace, and a hot tub! It was absolutely unbelievable!

The Baltimore TV stations came out and interviewed us as word spread about the tree house. They did a live remote broadcast by the fireplace and afterward B.G. slipped into the kitchenette and fixed lunch for the reporters and camera crew. There was some discussion about an appearance by B.G. on the Ed Sullivan Show, but ol' Eddie never got back to us on that one.

I became rather suspicious one day when this kid showed up and started asking a lot of questions about the tree house. I refused to let him tour the tree house, but B.G. insisted that we allow it. B.G. was so proud of his engineering marvel that he wanted everyone to see it, so I reluctantly gave in to the tour request. But I did not like this kid. There was just something about him that rubbed me the wrong way.

The kid was in there for only a few minutes before he unfolded a carpenter's rule (no retractable thirty-foot tape measures in those days) and started measuring every inch of the tree house! I was trying to figure out just what he was up to, and finally decided it was *not* something good. But B.G. just let the kid do as he pleased. When the kid finally prepared to leave, he looked at us and solemnly said, "Always use tools from Sears!"

Well, the next thing you know, this little copycat is building his *own* tree house…just like *ours*! I was outraged and asked Dominic about this kid. He said the kid was little Bobby Vila and would never amount to anything. Oh really? So I guess that's why the kid ended up with his own TV show on WBAL in Baltimore! The name of the show was *This Old Tree House*. Have you ever heard of anything so ridiculous?

I think Dominic was right and the kid never amounted to anything. I wonder what happened to him and all his tools from Sears?

BACK TO THE TREE HOUSE

I loved the tree house because it was a place of privacy and sanity. It allowed me an opportunity to escape from B.G. and his incessant over-achieving nature. The tree house was my place of solace, my oasis in the arid land called "B.G. World."

I had a lot of my games and toys up in the tree house. One of my favorites was the View Master, with the disks which were inserted and viewed in "3-D." It always fascinated me and I considered it to be one of the coolest toys ever invented!

I had numerous disks and I could view them for hours. I had *Bambi*, the *Lone Ranger*, *Peter Pan*...you name it and I had it. The most difficult thing was to keep my brother from bothering me when I wanted some "down time" to relax and enjoy the View Master. The kid could sure be one annoying pest when he was in the mood!

A bigger problem occurred when B.G. visited the tree house in my absence. He would then help himself to any and all of my toys and games, generally leaving them in disarray and sometimes in broken pieces. I seriously contemplated killing him on a number of occasions but decided against it. I hoped to one day graduate from high school and go on to college instead of acquiring a G.E.D. in a correctional facility.

B.G. found the View Master one day when I was not around and he proceeded to "tweak it." The next time I used it I found that it functioned as a Night Vision Device! It was incredible! I mean, even the *military* didn't have such a thing. B.G. had created a way for the View Master to amplify any available light (from the stars or moon) and make everything visible in the dark. I sat in the tree house at night and watched cats, rabbits, owls, deer, and anything else that liked to prowl in the dark. It was unbelievable!

Dominic came over one night and I told him to try out the "tweaked" View Master. He went nuts! He absolutely loved that thing. He really enjoyed sitting in the darkened tree house watching animals (and people) that could not see him. I found that he was especially fond of sitting in concealment while looking through Thelma Lou's bedroom window. The tree house put us right at eye-level with her second floor room and Dominic took full advantage of the situation. He told me that she would turn off all the lights in her room, undress, and then dance around naked!

Just the thought of seeing Thelma Lou naked was too much for me. I declined Dominic's offer to take a peek at her through the View Master. I really did not like to even look at her when she was *dressed*, and so I sure had no desire to see her naked! Also, the View Master got a *double* "tweaking" from B.G. because it *magnified* as well as provided night vision. Just think: a *close-up* of a naked Thelma Lou! Now *that's* the definition of pornography, I tell you!

Anyway, Thelma Lou's mother saw Dominic one night and told her husband. He went to Thelma Lou's room and glanced half-heartedly towards the tree house just to satisfy his

Don (age 9) and Ron (age 8), Baltimore, Maryland

wife. Dominic had already climbed down just as soon as he realized Thelma Lou's mother had spotted him, so there was no one for Mr. McGillicuddy to see. When Thelma Lou's parents went back downstairs to the living room Dominic could hear their conversation through an open window. It went something like this: "Yes, there *was* a boy there looking in her window. I saw him in that tree house. I'm sure it was *not* that nice little boy Ronald but probably his pervert older brother." The reply: "I didn't see anything and neither did you. Are you nuts? What boy wants to look at an ugly girl?" I'm sure that if Thelma Lou had any self-esteem issues they probably began at home.

I decided to give the View Master with the "enhanced optics" to Dominic, and I asked my parents for a new one the following Christmas. When they asked what happened to the old one, I told them that it "just disappeared one day."

DON'T TRY THIS AT HOME

One day I was watching TV up in the tree house when B.G. stepped off the elevator and asked for my Pez candy dispenser. Now back in those days Pez candies were very popular, but it was the totally cool dispensers that all the kids loved. I really did not want to give the Pez dispenser to B.G. because it was very likely that I would never see it again. Also, I was in the middle of some very serious cartoon-viewing.

Cartoons in those days (late 1950s and early 1960s) were absolutely the best! Nothing in the cartoon world has ever come close to the classics from that era. Remember *Rocky and Bullwinkle, Yogi Bear and Boo Boo, Huckleberry Hound*, and *Quick Draw McGraw*? They were great! Why, that old *Quick Draw McGraw* even had an alter ego known as *El Kabong*. I loved the character known as *El Kabong* because he was hilarious as a take-off on Zorro (and remember, Guy Williams was the one and only and best-ever Zorro, just like Clayton Moore as the original Lone Ranger). Senor Kabong did not use a gun or a whip, but preferred to bash the bad guys over the head with his guitar! I'm not sure if he ever actually played any music with the guitar or just used it as a non-lethal weapon. Anyway, *El Kabong* was one of my favorites as he righted wrongs, bashed bad guys, and rescued damsels in distress.

Today *El Kabong* would never make it. Why, some poor kid might be adversely affected by watching such antics, take his guitar to school, and hold an entire class of fifth-graders hostage! ("Call in S.W.A.T., he's got a guitar!") The "excessive violence" of *El Kabong* could lead to a gang of guitar-toting ten-year-olds forming a terrorist group to threaten national security! ("They've got twelve-string semi-automatic Stratocasters! Get the tear gas and the snipers ready!") Imagine the chaos at an airport. ("Slap the cuffs on that eighty-three-year old grandmother and get those nail clippers away from her, and do it quick! She's a small-time terrorist compared to her ten-year-old grandson! Why, the kid's packing a Martin *and* a ukulele!")

The other problem with *El Kabong* today would be the issue of ethnic stereotypes. Since he possessed an accent and hailed from "south of the border," the P.C.P.D. (Political Correctness Police Department) would have a field day! But they would also be upset with the "white bread" world of the *Hardy Boys* searching for the Applegate Treasure or *Spin and Marty* down on the ranch. Go figure!

All of this cartoon nostalgia has diverted me from the main story about B.G. and the Pez dispenser. I was unfazed by the violence-prone *El Kabong* and it was only coincidental that I threw the dispenser at B.G. and it hit him in the head. He yelped like a little puppy when I hit him so I gave him a "Mom-ism." That's one of those classic phrases that Mom used all the time when we misbehaved. This time I selected the following little gem: "Shut up or I'll really give you something to cry about!" It was the equivalent of Dad's "Don't make me come up there with my belt!" How about this one? "I will turn this car around right now and go right back home!" Or "Do you think I'm kidding, Mister? You just try me!" But I digress.

Little Whiner-Boy took the Pez dispenser and briefly dis-appeared, only to return in a matter of minutes with a gun! (I began to apologize to B.G. real fast!) But B.G. had no interest in revenge because he was in the creative mode. He had the Pez dispenser in one hand and Dad's .45 caliber semi-automat-ic pistol in the other hand. The pistol was from Dad's military service during WW II and it was kept in a locked case (which we were *never* to touch). Locks were no match for B.G., however, and Dad's rules were (in B.G.'s mind) made to be broken. Dad did not even have ammunition for the gun but this didn't matter to B.G. at all. He explained to me that the Pez dispenser was about the same size and shape as the pistol's ammunition clip. All that was required was a little "tweaking" (B.G.'s specialty) and then the pistol would (in theory) fire Pez candies. (Did Patton or MacArthur ever think about this?)

Well, the "tweaking" was quickly accomplished and there was no stopping B.G. from that point. The next thing I knew, B.G. popped in the Pez "clip" and cocked that baby. He fired off ten rounds of Pez candies faster than you could say, "N.R.A." and then went down the elevator. The candies made no sound as they were fired, but I heard "pop, pop, pop!" next door. I looked out of the tree house window and saw B.G., Dominic, and Tramp over in Thelma Lou's yard. She was screaming like crazy at B.G. and Dominic while a bunch of girls were running around in tears. It appeared that Thelma Lou was having some kind of fancy little tea party for some of her snooty girlfriends. B.G. and Dominic decided to use the festive balloons around Thelma Lou's yard for *target practice*! The candies had just enough velocity to pop the balloons, and the sound of the popping balloons was sufficient to scare Thelma Lou's guests into mass hysteria. In the midst of all this chaos was our dog, Tramp, calmly rooting through the balloon remnants and eating the tasty Pez candies within.

Thelma Lou's father had just gotten home from work about the time that the "B.G. Militia" went into action. He found broken balloons, screaming and crying girls, a wife who had fainted, my brother and Dominic trying to sneak away, and a very happy dog gobbling up the last of the Pez candies. Oh yeah, and the *pistol*! The sight of a gun in the vicinity of a bunch of kids was upsetting to Mr. McGillicuddy, to say the least. He threw water on his wife, told Thelma Lou and the rest of the girls to calm down, and then called the police. When they arrived, Mr. McGillicuddy told them everyone was OK. (Mrs. McGillicuddy had revived) and then sent them over to our house with "the evidence," Dad's pistol.

Dad had just gotten home from work when the police arrived. He said something like, "I wish I had to work overtime today" just as Mom said, "*Your* sons have been at it *again*!" (We were always *his* sons when we misbehaved and *Mom's* boys when we were good. As you can imagine, Mom rarely got to claim us.) Dad went ballistic when the cops showed him the pistol and told what had happened. "BOYS, come here right now!!!" he bellowed. Now B.G. and Dominic had joined me in the tree house where they were attempting to hide out from the long arm of the law. They could tell from the tone (not to mention the *volume*) of Dad's voice that he was ready to commit some serious child abuse. So the little felons decided to respond to Dad's command by heading down from the tree house and joining him, Mom, and the cops (no use making things worse by forcing Dad to go looking for them). Dad's first question was, "Where's your brother?"

Now, isn't that just what you would expect? I mean, why should *I* possibly get off when I had nothing to do with this incident? Based on all you've read so far, is it any wonder that Dad and Mom would just naturally assume that I had to be involved? My situation was always this: Guilty until proven innocent. In the case of B.G. it was usually: Innocent even after a preponderance of the evidence indicated guilt beyond a reasonable doubt. (I also watched a lot of *Perry Mason* as well as the cartoons.)

Dad walked around to the back of the house and stood below the tree house. "Down here NOW, Boy!" Mom, B.G., Dominic, and the police all gathered around as I exited from the tree house elevator and got snagged by Dad. B.G. and Dominic saw their opportunity to blame *me* for this latest transgression so that they could avoid punishment, or at least implicate me so that I had to share their penalty. So they started in on me, telling Dad that *I* got the pistol and decided to ruin Thelma Lou's party. Their version seemed to totally omit their involvement. Dominic even claimed that he had been training as a *paramedic* and only went to Thelma Lou's house to render first aid to the wounded. Dad got madder by the minute and Mom began to wail, "He's destined for the penitentiary, I tell you!" My situation seemed to be deteriorating while Dominic and B.G. started to grin smugly. Just when it looked as if I was headed to Reform School (one cop had already pulled out his handcuffs) the "Cavalry" arrived!

Thelma Lou and her parents heard all the commotion at our house so they decided to join the party. Thelma Lou let B.G. and Dominic have it…and good! She told them off and even *slapped* B.G.! Her mother restrained Thelma Lou and then told my parents and the cops that I had absolutely *nothing* to do with the aforementioned incident. Mrs. McGillicuddy had personally seen B.G. fire the pistol from the tree house and heard B.G. and Dominic laughing about the situation. Mr. McGillicuddy stated that Dominic looked like a "Peeping Tom" seen hanging around the tree house recently. He never really liked Dominic, and with good reason. The situation had started looking pretty good for me, but pretty bleak for Dominic and B.G. (A.K.A.—"The Sniper" and "The Assassin"). Dad and Mom actually apologized to me before they and the cops hauled off B.G. and Dominic. Thelma Lou's parents left, but not before I thanked them repeatedly and offered to mow their lawn for free all summer. I was all alone in the back yard with Thelma Lou (scary!) and she started to make "goo-goo" eyes at me. This frightened me more than the big cop with handcuffs!

Thelma Lou smiled and finally spoke. "Guess I saved your cute butt that time, didn't I?" I didn't know what to say except, "Thanks, I guess I owe you one." Thelma Lou cuddled up real close, wrapped her arms around my neck, and put her lips to my ear. Then she softly whispered, "Oh sweetie, you certainly *do* owe me…big time! You have no idea! Just make sure you remember that when I come to collect!" Then she let me go and walked toward her house, pausing only long enough to turn and blow me a kiss.

I ran toward the police car as fast as I could, determined to implicate myself so that I could go to jail, be placed in protective custody, or something. I really had no desire to remain free so that Thelma Lou could sneak up on me one day and demand that I become her Boy Toy!

CONSPIRACY THEORY

Do you remember the slide rule? It was big in the days before calculators and electronic computers, and was (at least in my school) a required skill. If you've ever seen the movie *Apollo 13* starring Tom Hanks, then you've seen slide rules. During a crucial point in the movie the scientists back on earth have to perform a number of complex mathematical calculations. They have no calculators or computers; instead, they do the calculations with slide rules.

I hated the slide rule and could never get anywhere with it. Actually, I hated anything that had to do with math, period. B.G. was, of course, a mathematical wizard who delighted in performing advanced mathematical calculations. It was like a game to him and he was never intimidated by anything mathematical. My mother insisted that he help me since I struggled so with math, and B.G. was kind enough to *try* to help. I also think that he secretly delighted in seeing me struggle with math problems that were, to him, mere child's play. I would get so angry because, even with B.G.'s help, I just could *not* comprehend the stuff. So then either I or B.G. (or both of us) would storm off, Mom would just throw up her hands in disgust, my work would remain undone (or done wrong), and I would continue my pathetic "D minus" existence.

I really had no use for a slide rule. If I could figure out how to cut a pepperoni pizza in half I was satisfied. Who cares about the cosine of pi divided by the logarithm of a leap year anyway? But B.G., well that was a different story altogether. He *loved* the slide rule! When he was in fifth grade he tutored twelfth graders in calculus! He could do calculations so fast that he made the slide rule *smoke*! He amazed everyone and made me look pathetic. I used the slide rule as a "walkie-talkie" when Dominic and I played Army. The center slide would be raised as the antenna and I would say things like, "Roger, over and out." (Who was that "Roger" guy, anyway?)

My brother ridiculed me for using the slide rule as a toy when it was actually a "sophisticated instrument for precise mathematical calculations." (Oh please, give me a break!)

I decided one day that I had heard enough from little Mr. Slide Rule so it was high time for *me* to do a little "tweaking" of my own. B.G. had just returned from Cape Canaveral where he instructed the NASA engineers in Advanced Slide Rule Applications. I told him that his slide rule probably needed some cleaning since he had used it so much with the NASA guys. B.G. was suspicious, but Mom urged him to "let your brother do something nice for you." (Man, was she gullible at times!) So off I went to the basement with the slide rule. I found Dad's can of WD 40 and I oiled that baby up good! I mean, we're talking serious lubrication! I wiped off the excess oil, put the slide rule in its special protective case, and returned it to B.G. in a ceremonial manner. He was still suspicious but never even looked at the slide rule, nor did he remove it from the case. He muttered (at Mom's insistence) a half-hearted "Thank you" and went off to bed. So far, so good.

We had, by this time, moved from Baltimore up to Harford County. The "gang" managed to stay intact because Dominic was also there. His father and uncle had an extended lay-off from Bethlehem Steel in Baltimore. Tired of the strikes and lay-offs, they decided to pursue their life-long dream of opening a pizza and sub shop. So they jumped at the chance to purchase the "Capri Shop" when it came up for sale in Bel Air. Thelma Lou also joined us because her father left the *Baltimore Sun* to become the editor of Bel Air's local paper, the *Aegis*. Her mother secured a job as the assistant principal at Bel Air Junior High School. So we all continued to live in close proximity in Harford County rather than in Baltimore. We resided in the country a few miles outside the sleepy little town of Bel Air. The day after I lubricated B.G.'s slide rule was a big day for him, as well as the school and the entire town. B.G. was scheduled to give a demonstration of his slide rule prowess before the entire school. His trip to NASA had put the town of Bel Air "on the map" and B.G. had been featured in an article in the *Aegis*. Now the *Baltimore Sun* and WBAL-TV wanted in on the action. Everybody had to have a piece of the Wonder Child! It just made me want to puke!

The big day arrived and everyone was there: reporters, radio and TV crews, the mayor of Bel Air, the governor of Maryland, NASA officials, and some military officers…you name it and they were there. There was initially a lot of fanfare and praise of B.G. (Oh, please!), then the action started. B.G. was to compete for speed and accuracy against a Bel Air High School senior (Tomiko Watanabe) and a NASA engineer (Rajiv Gupta). They were given a series of difficult and highly complex calculations to perform, and this was B.G.'s opportunity to "strut his stuff." WBAL-TV broadcast the event live. I mean, this was really a big deal!

B.G. was so cocky and confident that he gave the other two a head start. He waited *three minutes* before he even removed the slide rule from its case! Then he whipped it out and started "sliding" at lightning speed. This was just too much for an overly-lubricated slide rule. The next thing I knew, the center slide came flying out of that thing and shot across the Bel Air Elementary School stage! It nailed the governor right between the eyes and ricocheted over towards General Thomas of NASA. He was a military man with combat experience; thus, he was much more prepared than the governor. The general yelled, "Incoming!" and dove under his chair. The errant "missile" then hit our school principal, Mrs. Fitzsimmons, in the temple and knocked her out cold. At this point Dominic arose and led the student body in a standing ovation for B.G. while the school choir sang, "Ding dong, the witch is dead." It was a scene of utter chaos!

Order was finally restored after the paramedics finished treating the wounded. The vice-principal then went over to the microphone and announced that school would be dismissed early. The students cheered and B.G. became an instant hero. He was able to K.O. the school principal (even *I* had to admire him for that) and get everyone out of school early, all in the space of a few minutes! My plan to embarrass him had totally backfired.

Some of the students hoisted B.G. onto their shoulders and triumphantly carried him out of the school auditorium, but not before I stood up and yelled, "It's Not Fair!" Everyone stopped and stood silently as I explained that *I* oiled the slide rule and set off a chain of events resulting in early dismissal from school. *I* should be the one carried out, *not* B.G. the Wonder Boy. Suddenly, all the students began to laugh and someone yelled, "You're pathetic! Only your brother could think of something like this!" (The voice sounded strangely like that of Dominic.) None of the students believed me.

The vice-principal, mayor, general, and governor *did* believe me, however, and I *did* get carried out of the auditorium (by the *police*). I was promptly taken to the office and my parents were contacted. The film from the WBAL-TV camera crew was confiscated and presented as evidence. The entire incident, including my "confession," had been captured on film. The F.B.I. interviewed me to determine if I had plotted to assassinate the governor, general, and the rest. I explained that I had merely tried to embarrass my over-achieving brother but never anticipated that things would turn out as they did. My parents confirmed the sibling rivalry between us, my jealousy, sense of inferiority, and my need for psychiatric help.

The result of all this was better than anticipated. All criminal charges were dropped and I did *not* (despite what my brother and Dominic said) end up with a "rap sheet" or jail time. I was suspended from school for two weeks and "grounded" at home for two months. I had to mow Mrs. Fitzsimmons' yard all summer long…for FREE! I had to apologize to the mayor, governor, and general. And get this: Dominic's parents would NOT allow *him* to play with *me* for the entire summer! The kid later voted as "Most Likely to Commit a Felony" had to stay away from *me* because I was a "bad influence." Do you believe it? B.G. had won…again!

THAT OLD TIME RELIGION

I remember one summer when things got interesting because a new kid moved into our Harford County neighborhood. The kid was Jewish and his name was Aaron.

Aaron's entrance into the neighborhood was the catalyst for our big discussion about religion. We asked Aaron to tell us about Judaism; afterward, we decided that each day one of "the gang" would talk about his particular religion. Now, you've *never* heard a religious debate until you've heard a group of eleven and twelve year-olds discussing the subject (heatedly, at times) in a tree house! (This was our first "order of business" when we moved to the new neighborhood…build a new super-deluxe tree house.)

The next day Dominic told us about Catholicism, and that really created a major debate! The following day it was my turn so I spoke about Presbyterianism and the doctrine of predestination. This became so controversial that we almost had a fight (talk about a bunch of zealots!) and someone wisely suggested that we end the discussion and just "play church." I'm sure that you can imagine how things went after this idiotic decision. It was like the Crusades and the Inquisition all rolled into one!

Dominic took the lead on "playing church," insisting that we all be Catholics while he served as our "priest." B.G. brought some Wonder Bread and Welch's Grape Juice out of the house and Dominic proceeded to serve "communion." I was hungry since it was almost lunchtime so I asked "Father Dominic" if he could serve some bologna sandwiches instead of those little tiny pieces of bread. He then threatened to *excommunicate* me if I made any more remarks.

B.G. spoke up about this time and said that he had been reading about Catholicism. He believed that my rude behavior toward "Father D" (OK, so we were a progressive congregation with little use for formality) was the result of *demonic possession.* Furthermore, it was B.G.'s firm belief that an *exorcism* by "Father D" was in order. My loving brother was not ready to quit at this point. He went on to state that he had also been reading up on Judaism. He was positive that I was an "uncircumcised Philistine" who needed some work done by "Rabbi Aaron." My situation was not looking good at all! The resident Baptist, Thelma Lou, decided it was time for her to depart.

The "priest" and the "rabbi" debated on what should happen first: the exorcism or the circumcision (either way I was bound to lose). I frantically looked around for a quick exit out of the tree house but B.G. was watching me like a hawk. Just as soon as I tried to make my move he yelled, "Bind that infidel!" so Dominic and Aaron grabbed me and quickly tied me to a chair. B.G. pulled out his Swiss Army knife and said that *he* voted for the "rabbi" to go first. I was desperate and had to think fast, so I asked for a moment to speak on my behalf (no one else, especially my own brother, was going to plead for me).

Now B.G. knew that I was just stalling for time, but Aaron and Dominic out-voted him and agreed to let me speak. I told them that the Catholic and Jewish positions were represented but *not* the Presbyterian one. Since B.G. (my Presbyterian kin) was determined to see me burn at the stake (among other things), I felt that he was biased and therefore could *not* fairly represent the Presbyterian position. Dominic, Aaron, and B.G. were getting very restless and told me that I had to come up with some "Presbyterian stuff" real fast!

This was the chance I'd been waiting for, and I took full advantage of it. I yelled, "Point of order!" and they all just stared at me. Then I said, "I call for the question," and they stared some more, looked at each other, and shook their heads. Finally I screamed, "I want to amend the previous motion!" and Dominic and Aaron looked at each other with bewilderment and shrugged their shoulders. B.G. yelled, "I told you he was demon-possessed! Off with his foreskin!" (I still wonder what this kid was reading back then.) I decided to try my final appeal: "I move that we take no action at this time but instead form a committee to study this matter." Aaron and Dominic were so confounded by this time that they untied me and allowed me to leave the tree house (even *without* a "second," discussion, or vote).

B.G. was livid! "I can't believe you two fell for that!" he screamed. He almost got me that time and, as always, would have been blameless since he manipulated Aaron and Dominic to do his "dirty work." We were reluctant to "play church" after that, especially since the parents found out what happened (and *almost* happened). I decided that I would remain a lifelong Presbyterian since the committees, motions, etc. take up a lot of time but *do* seem to serve a purpose. I mean, when was the last time anyone got circumcised or exorcised at the General Assembly? I also decided that even though the other kids were carrying slingshots and Swiss Army knives around with them, I would be safer (and better served) by carrying *Robert's Rules of Order*.

THE REVIVAL MEETING

Well, there was another time that I recall when we "played church." A new kid, Sammy, visited the neighborhood one summer. He was Thelma Lou's cousin from Lynchburg, Virginia. Sammy was a Baptist who went to a church pastored by a preacher named Jerry Falwell. He came to the tree house with Thelma Lou and announced that he would be holding a "revival meeting." The Catholic (Dominic), Presbyterians (B.G. and me), and the Jewish guy (Aaron) did not know what to make of this. Dominic asked him, "If you're a Baptist, shouldn't your name be John?" Sammy was unruffled by Dominic's insult and replied, "Where do *you* go to church?" Dominic's response: "The Immaculate Shrine of St. Bartholomew's Chapel of the Nativity of the Holy Name of the Virgin Mary." Sammy's disdain was evident. "Oh, so you're a *Catholic*?" Dominic bristled and said, "You know Sammy…you could just disappear one day." Sammy countered, "I'm not ready to discuss the rapture yet." Thelma Lou knew that Sammy had "crossed the line" with Dominic. Trouble was brewing fast, so Thelma Lou asked Sammy to talk about baptism. Preacher Boy Sammy jumped on this faster than a televangelist asking for money. This distracted Dominic and gave him a chance to "cool down."

"Baptism consists of immersion in water…" said Sammy, "and I'm ready to baptize every heathen in this tree house." "Who are you calling heathen, Preacher Boy?" yelled Dominic. Thelma Lou looked at me ("Do something!") and then at Sammy ("Do you have a death wish?"). I said, "Enough yelling and fussing! Mom and Dad will be up here if you guys don't settle down." This really calmed things down since the thought of parental intervention was as welcome as a plague of locusts spewing fire and brimstone. Dominic told Sammy that he (Dominic) was baptized as a baby and B.G. and I said the same thing. "You can't baptize babies," wailed

Sammy, "they don't even know what's going on." "Sure you can…" replied Dominic, "you sprinkle or pour the water on their head." Sammy was livid, "NO, NO, NO!" He definitely had his work cut out for him in this revival. Sammy said that baptism was by immersion ONLY. "You've got to put them all the way *under* the water or it doesn't count!" More arguments ensued.

B.G. had been sitting quietly through all of this. His eyes were dancing, though, and I knew he was up to something. "Hold it, hold it," he said, "let's try out this baptism stuff and see what works. Who wants to be the heathen?" No one volunteered since no one really trusted B.G. Plus, all of us (except Aaron) had already been baptized. "OK, we'll need someone else," said B.G. "Tramp, here boy. Come here, Tramp!" Now Tramp was the stray dog we had adopted. He was part Beagle, part mutt, part flea haven…but *not* stupid. As soon as B.G. and the rest of us climbed down from the tree house, Tramp knew something was amiss. When B.G. started running water from the hose into our old plastic wading pool, Tramp took off like he was shot out of a cannon! B.G. wasn't happy. "Well, I guess we won't baptize that stupid mutt." B.G. was always creative and started looking around until his eyes fell upon Thelma Lou's Barbie doll. "Hey, Barbie needs to be baptized!" Thelma Lou sprang into action. "Don't you touch her!" But B.G. was too fast. He had Barbie submerged faster than you could say *Sea Hunt* (remember that show?). Bubbles were coming out of Barbie everywhere as she rapidly filled with water. B.G. slyly looked at Sammy, "Hey, Rev. Sam. Is this how you do it?" Thelma Lou was going berserk. "Stop him, Sammy, stop him! He's drowning Barbie!" Sammy shrieked, "You're holding her under water for too long!" B.G. replied, "Maybe so, but she's got a lot of sin to wash away. Didn't you see how the little tramp was acting around the Ken doll? She needs to stay under for a while longer." Now Aaron had seen enough. "G.I. Joe will save her!" he yelled. G.I. Joe had his frogman outfit on and Aaron plunged him into the water. Dominic was not upset by any of this chaos. He smiled at B.G. and asked, "Did you know that you're touching Barbie's boobies?" Sammy yelled at Dominic for "profaning the sacrament" by using the word "boobies" during the baptism. I asked, "What are boobies?"

Finally, B.G. brought Barbie up. "Sister Barbie, you are cleansed!" He handed the doll (wet boobies and all) to a hysterical Thelma Lou. She screamed, "You're insane!" at B.G. before tearfully running away with a still-dripping Barbie. Sammy started to speak but B.G. cut him off. "See, that immersion stuff is no good. Suppose that had been a real baby!" Sammy was now "over the edge." He lunged toward B.G. and pushed him backward into the wading pool. B.G. screamed when he landed in the cold water and screamed again when G.I. Joe's spear gun poked him in the butt. "Ow…Oww… Owww! Help me, help me. I think I'm being attacked by a shark!" Now Aaron was upset because G.I. Joe was getting "crushed to death." He jumped into the pool and pulled B.G. off of G.I. Joe while yelling, "If he's broken, you'll pay to replace him!" Then Aaron stormed off leaving me, Dominic, and Sammy to watch B.G. flounder in the wading pool. "Get me out of here…I can't swim!" screeched B.G. "You don't have to swim, moron, you just have to stand up," said Dominic. I chimed in, "You would think that a kid with an I.Q. of 210 could figure out a wading pool!" Dominic was now laughing hysterically. "Your brother and I are not certified lifeguards. Sorry, but we are not authorized to help you." Sammy began to speak in a sing-song preacher's voice about "Divine retribution on backsliders." Just about this time Tramp returned. He took one look at B.G., trotted over to the wading pool, and started drinking. "Good boy, Tramp. I knew you would save me," said B.G. But the wonder dog Tramp had other ideas. He cocked his head from side to side and then cocked his leg. He peed all over B.G. and I mean *all* over. Then he barked twice, smiled his doggie smile (as if to say, "I've been divinely appointed to do a little baptizing of my own") and ran off. Dominic and I fell to the ground and began to laugh so hard that we could barely breathe. Sammy smiled and began to walk away. He stopped after a few steps and turned around to address a soggy B.G. "You know, I think you guys are right. Tramp just convinced me that *sprinkling* is the best way to baptize." Laughing as he departed, Sammy announced, "I proclaim this revival a success!"

THE FIELD TRIP

Nothing was more fun than a school field trip. Anytime I could get *out* of school (legally) was a happy time. So I loved field trips, and the best one was our trip from Bel Air down to the Baltimore Zoo.

The zoo was certainly better than something boring—like an art museum. The zoo trip allowed a bunch of wild kids to have an opportunity to run around among their peers—Wild Animals! The teachers and adult chaperones were convinced that the wrong group was caged, although some of our group did (years later) end up behind bars.

Getting there was half the fun. We piled onto the bus with a sense of excitement because a field trip was an adventure! Everyone had their lunch packed, permission slip signed, souvenir money tucked away and snacks close at hand. Things went well as long as we all behaved. The teachers were more relaxed, we were allowed to eat snacks during the bus ride, and usually we sang a bunch of silly songs.

Dominic was the one who "pushed the limits" during a field trip. He *always* took over one of the back seats (away from the teacher's watchful eyes) and made sure that the prettiest girl on the bus was sitting beside him. This was OK until Dominic had her sitting on his *lap* (which usually happened before we got out of the school parking lot). At this point, teacher intervention was guaranteed. The "cutie" had to sit up front with the teacher and, you guessed it, *I* had to go back and sit with Dominic. Now don't misunderstand—I liked Dominic. We were friends and spent lots of time together. But on a field trip I just wanted to "fly under the radar" and avoid any trouble. I wanted to enjoy the time away from school as much as I could. My goal was to behave and have fun without hearing a teacher or chaperone call my name the entire day. Making me sit with Dominic, however, was *not* the way to avoid trouble.

We weren't even out of Harford County before Dominic grew tired of the singing. I thought that "Row, Row, Row Your Boat" sung in rounds sounded pretty good. But not to Dominic! He wanted to sing "Louie, Louie" and asked me to join in with him (actually, he put my arm in a "hammer lock" and gently persuaded me). I had barely gotten the first "Louie" out of my mouth before one of the chaperones (our minister's wife) grabbed me, put my *other* arm in a "hammer lock," and said in her sternest Presbyterian voice, "That will be enough of that, young man!" (You always knew it was a major transgression if someone called you by your first *and* middle name or called you "young man.") She then marched me halfway up the aisle to a vacant seat beside, you guessed it, Thelma Lou!

Thelma Lou was still in love with me—madly in love with me! I still despised her and always did my best to avoid her. I wanted to give the girl *no* encouragement whatsoever, but the chaperone's intervention ruined all that. "Oh, Donnie," Thelma Lou cooed, "how nice that you wanted to sit with me." She said this loud enough that *everyone* on the bus could hear it! I could hear Dominic snickering and I thought to myself, "He could just disappear one day." Thelma Lou was now trying to snuggle up to me as Dominic started to sing "This Girl is a Woman Now" (by Gary Puckett and the Union Gap). I turned and glared at Dominic just before the "music censor" put her hand over his mouth.

We had not even reached the Baltimore County line and already I'd been in three different seats! And this last one, beside Thelma Lou, was the worst yet. She continued to "sweet talk" me as everyone on the bus watched and listened. I looked at B.G. with pleading eyes and whispered, "Sing something." I knew Thelma Lou was not going to shut up so I figured that the singing would at least drown her out. B.G. said, "No problem, Bro. I'll help you out." He then stood up and said, "It's time for a little bit of that sweet soul music from the Temptations." B.G. launched into an off-key rendition of "My Girl" (*not* the song I would have preferred at this point in time), and everyone on the bus joined in. And when they came to the "My Girl" refrain, everyone stood and pointed at me and Thelma Lou! I turned crimson and slid down into the seat as far as I possibly could. Thelma Lou cozied up as close as possible and whispered, "Donnie, it's *our* song!" Man, that was one very long bus ride!

We finally arrived at the zoo and I shot out of the bus and away from Thelma Lou as fast as I could go. I smacked B.G. on the back of the head as I ran by, reminding him that his song selection would result in "payback." The teacher saw this and told me that my parents would be informed of my "assault" on my brother. This day was going downhill fast. I had such high hopes for this field trip but, so far, everything had gone wrong. Of course, the day was not over yet.

"Gather around, students, so I can give you a few reminders," said the teacher. This went on for about thirty-five minutes! (You know the routine.) "Don't run, don't hit, don't wander off, don't annoy the animals, don't have any FUN (OK, I made that up), listen to the zoo guide, etc., etc., etc." I was thinking to myself, "Give us a break, lady! We just had a one-and-a-half hour bus ride! Just let us go pee and then see the animals!" The last reminder was the killer: "Stay in pairs." And *who* were you paired up with? Why, your seat mate on the bus! I dropped to my knees and began to sob uncontrollably. Thelma Lou came over, kneeled down, and put her arm around me. "Yes, my sweet. Spending the entire day together makes me want to shed tears of joy also." As she helped me to my feet and intertwined her arm in mine, I looked over at B.G. Somehow his partner for the day was…"Cutie Pie!!!" How did he do it? And what about Dominic? Oh, this was even better! Since he had misbehaved on the bus he had to partner up with a *teacher*! But not just any teacher—Oh no. Dominic was assigned to Miss Goodbody, our gorgeous student teacher. (That was her name—*really*—I'm not making this up.) Miss Goodbody had blonde hair, blue eyes, and curves in places where most girls don't even have places. She was twenty-one and looked like a model! Every guy in school was in love with her. So *this* was Dominic's "punishment" for misbehaving on the bus??? She put her arm around Dominic's shoulders and said, "You'll be a good boy for *me*, won't you?" And Dominic (in the voice he probably used in the confessional booth with the priest) replied, "Oh yes, Miss Goodbody. I'll behave as long as I'm close to you." He then winked at me. I thought I was going to puke. So off we went to tour the zoo, B.G. and Dominic with the "super models" and me with the "Anti-model." Where was that "Extreme Makeover" show back then?

Now a lot of the zoo animals were not that exciting. Most of us wanted to see the Big Stuff—lions, tigers, elephants, giraffes, and gorillas. So the building with the big cats was a real treat. We all crowded around to watch the lions, panthers, leopards, and tigers. Everything went well until we got to the tiger cage. That's when nature took its course and things got …well…quite interesting. It seems that one of the lady tigers was in a receptive mood to Mr. Tiger's advances. The next thing we knew, old Mr. Tiger was getting *real* friendly with the aforementioned lady tiger. Some of the kids snickered, some turned away with a look of disgust, and others just stared in wonder ("What the heck is going on in that cage?"). I had *no* idea what I was watching, but Thelma Lou apparently did. She smiled, squeezed my hand, and said, "ROWRRR!" At that particular moment, I wasn't sure if the tiger or Thelma Lou frightened me the most. Dominic ("Mr. Precocious") knew exactly what was going on and yelled, "Go tiger…You're the man!" B.G. (with "Cutie Pie" in tow) looked at me and whispered, "The Rolling Stones." He then began to sing, loudly and off-key (which was the *only* way I ever heard my brother sing), "I can't get no…satisfaction!" The teachers and chaperones arrived, took one look at Mr. Tiger's antics, and hastily moved us along to another venue.

We enjoyed the elephants, hippos, giraffes, and reptiles, along with various other animals. We behaved and all the animals behaved. We saw no more impromptu "facts of life" lessons during the remainder of the day. We ate lunch, relaxed for a while, and then prepared for the big finale prior to our return to school. The big finale was, of course, the Monkey House!

I guess the Monkey House was our favorite because the monkeys were most like us. They did all the same stuff that we did. They jumped around and acted crazy, made funny faces and lots of noise, and picked lice off each other. (I just threw in that last part to see if you were paying attention!) We loved them all: spider monkeys, howler monkeys, orangutans, chimpanzees, and...GORILLAS! The last stop was the best one because it had the gorillas. They were great! We all jumped around and did our best gorilla noises and impersonations. We yelled, "Me Tarzan, You Cheetah!" We gave the gorillas nicknames (King Kong, Mighty Joe Young, Yo' Mama) and did our best to irritate them enough to get a response. And we finally *did* get a response from the "Alpha male" whose zoo name was Thor (we called him "Bubba").

Now, you have to remember that in those days (the 1960s) people were not as safety-conscious (or prone to sue) as they are today. You could drive without seatbelts, buy firecrackers and handguns almost anywhere, and get "up close and personal" with a gorilla. (You could *not*, however, run with scissors.) The gorilla cage had a set of bars to contain the gorilla and another set of bars outside to contain the people. The distance from one set of bars to the other set was approximately four feet. There was *no* impenetrable barrier of bullet-resistant, gorilla-resistant, super space-age unbreakable safety glass. At the time everyone thought that this was OK because signs were conspicuously posted on the outer bars which read: "If you stick your hand through these bars the gorilla will rip it off and eat it!" No, actually the sign read: "Caution! For your personal safety and the safety of the gorillas, do NOT reach through the bars!" That was it!!! Now, I was always confused about the "safety of the gorillas" part. I mean, what could *we* do to a 400-pound gorilla? (OK, we could have—*hypothetically*, of course—thrown some peanuts through the bars which hit the gorilla and made him mad.) Let me just say that if you *ignore* the warning about the "safety of the gorillas" by hitting a gorilla with peanuts, then you better *heed* the warning about *your* safety!

Bubba responded to our provocative acts by first trying to stare us down and we foolishly stared back. And as you know, the *last* thing you want to do in the animal kingdom (unless you're prepared for "Smackdown") is to stare back. Instead, you should show submissiveness by looking away from the animal (which means that you don't see the first punch coming). We were not up on our Animal Etiquette (see Emily Post's *How to Avoid Having a Gorilla Beat the Crap Out of You*) so we just stared and stared. Bubba got even more irritated and probably contemplated the idea of opening up a big old can of "Jungle Whup-Ass" on us. It was not a good situation for us, but we were a bunch of stupid kids.

Now you have to understand something: Gorillas are *very* strong! Did you know that a little old *chimp* has the strength of three grown men? So how strong do you think a GORILLA might be? Why, gorillas send their *kids* out before breakfast to beat up a bunch of chimps—just for the fun of it! So antagonizing a 400-pound gorilla is just about the stupidest thing you can do! But we did it.

Bubba was not only big and strong—he was mean! He was an ape with attitude. Bubba came to the Baltimore Zoo by way of the Bronx Zoo in New York City. And you could tell it. He had that NY swagger and that NY attitude. When they sent him to the Baltimore Zoo he got angry, just as if he'd been traded to the Orioles from the Yankees. Bubba had the proverbial "chip on his shoulder" because, in his mind, he'd been demoted and sent to the minor leagues. He considered himself superior to the Baltimore gorillas. He despised "Charm City" as inferior to the "Big Apple." So when we threw peanuts and yelled at him, Bubba stared back as if to say, "You talkin' to me?" He wore a "I Love NY" sweatshirt and had a certain newspaper article prominently posted on the wall in his cage. The article concerned the defeat of the Baltimore Colts by the New York Jets in Super Bowl III. (OUCH!!!) This ape was cocky, no doubt about it. But you're only cocky if you can't back it up, and Bubba could. He was a fuzzy force to be reckoned with, and we would soon see the errors of our ways. (Did you know that gorillas send their young to NYC to toughen them up? It's like "Gorilla Boot Camp.")

When Bubba had taken all of the abuse from us that he could tolerate, he let out a loud roar. This so frightened Thelma Lou that she dropped her purse through the outer bars. Without hesitation, she reached in to retrieve it and put herself in easy reach of Bubba's grasp. Actually, we *all* were—even when outside the bars. Remember that four-foot "safety barrier" between the inner and outer bars? BIG DEAL! A gorilla's arms are at least SIX feet long! Bubba could have reached out and put a choke hold on any one of us at any time. He was just toying with us. He was a sly one, that's for sure.

Back to Thelma Lou. She grabbed the strap of her purse and began to pull, but Bubba grabbed the purse itself. "Gimme my purse, you stupid monkey!" she screamed. Bubba ignored her and just kept pulling the purse closer, which brought Thelma Lou's arm nearer to him. "Let go, Thelma Lou!" screamed B.G., the teachers, and every kid in sight. I didn't say anything but instead grabbed Thelma Lou and pulled her backwards (but not before Bubba grabbed her wrist). "Aieee!" screamed everyone. "The gorilla's going to eat her!" screamed one of the chaperones. So there we were. Thelma Lou was firmly in Bubba's grasp as he ransacked her purse. Thelma Lou began to cry hysterically. (Now, in defense of Bubba, I have to tell you something. Thelma Lou later revealed that she was most upset about losing her purse. She was scared but not in pain. Bubba never squeezed her wrist or hurt her—he just held on for a while. I think the poor gorilla was just lonely. Can I get a refrain of "My Girl," please?) Another thing to consider was this: Earlier, Thelma Lou was the *only* kid who yelled at the peanut throwers for "tormenting the poor sweet gorilla" and I think Bubba was appreciative. I don't believe he ever had any intention of harming Thelma Lou (but he would have ripped the arms off of a few peanut throwers, I'll bet). He was just curious about the purse…and lonely. (*Very* lonely, if you ask me. I mean, c'mon gorilla, it's Thelma Lou! If he'd grabbed onto "Cutie Pie" or Miss Goodbody I would have understood. But Thelma Lou???) Anyway, being in the grasp of a 400-pound gorilla, even a lovesick and lonely gorilla, is pretty scary. No one knew what to do. No one except Dominic.

While kids screamed and cried, teachers fainted, and zoo guides poked at Bubba with big sticks (yeah, that really calmed him down), Dominic sprang into action. He reached through the outer bars and grabbed the *gorilla's* wrist. Bubba was so surprised that he let Thelma Lou go but he just glared at Dominic. And Dominic glared right back! I yelled, "No, Dominic! Are you crazy?" but Dominic just squeezed the gorilla's wrist even harder as he tried to stare Bubba down. B.G. screamed, "Dominic, let go. Thelma Lou is free!" But Dominic ignored him as he squeezed the gorilla's wrist even harder and stared at Bubba without blinking.

And then I remembered: Dominic lived in New York before moving to Maryland. He knew the New York attitude better than Bubba! The "in your face" attitude. The "never back down" mentality. But even better than that—Dominic's family was *Sicilian*! The next thing I knew, Dominic muttered, "You could just disappear, you ugly ape!" (He also did some trash-talking about the gorilla's momma, but I can't include that here.) And then (and I'm not making this up) the gorilla looked away! Dominic had dominated and stared Bubba down! Dominic was the new "Alpha male" (not that I ever doubted that anyway). Big Bad Bubba had finally met his match. He looked at his wrist as if to say, "Please let me go," but Dominic held on. "I want all of the stuff from the purse," said Dominic in a low voice. Bubba complied without hesitation. Thelma Lou's comb, change purse, bobby pins, gum, feminine hygiene products, hairbrush, lipstick (no problem with Bubba returning this since it was not his shade)—everything was gently tossed over the bars to Thelma Lou by Bubba. Then Dominic gave him one more glare, released his grip on Bubba's wrist, and slowly turned and walked away.

Everyone just stood there dumbfounded. We could not believe what we had just witnessed. Only Thelma Lou spoke. "Thank you, Dominic. You saved my life," she said in a trembling voice. Dominic never replied but just kept walking toward the bus. Bubba sat quietly in his tire swing rubbing his sore wrist. We filed out one by one and followed Dominic onto the bus, but not before B.G. grinned at Bubba and whispered, "Who's your daddy?"

The first part of the ride was pretty quiet, but gradually everyone perked up. Thelma Lou was OK and Dominic was a hero. The teachers agreed that we could stop at a Gino's for some hamburgers (named for the Baltimore Colts great, Gino Marchetti, and not to be confused with Ameche's). The food seemed to be just what we needed, and everyone was pretty lively as we settled back in the bus for the remainder of the ride home. Miss Goodbody told Dominic, "That was the bravest thing I've ever seen," and *she* then proceeded to sit on his *lap* all the way home. I had hoped that Thelma Lou would park beside Dominic and express her undying gratitude, but that was too much to ask. You guessed it…She snuggled up beside *me* again and sighed softly, "Oh Donnie, what an adventure we've had today! Just think about telling this to our *children* one day." Everyone on the bus heard this and started yelling and laughing. I wanted to jump out of the bus window, crawl under the seat…anything to get away from Thelma Lou! Since she had the "gorilla death grip" on my hand, I knew escape was impossible. I heard Miss Goodbody giggle. I saw "Cutie Pie" wiggle (up close to B.G.). And here I was stuck with the "Anti-model" who, most recently, was almost going steady with Bubba the gorilla! (He *did* take her to our Senior Prom in 1968.) I couldn't win no matter what happened. I just put my face against the bus window and began to cry as B.G. softly sang the Temptation's hit "I Wish it Would Rain." I thought to myself, Maybe I should just drop out of school, marry Thelma Lou (get it over with), and go live in a trailer somewhere. Or join the Army…or the circus…or the French Foreign Legion.

NOT A CREATURE WAS STIRRING

Women seem to do some strange things as their kids grow up. One of those things is collecting stuff. It's as if the care of the "stuff" meets a basic need. Since the kids are older and need less care and attention, the "stuff" gets the attention (so the need to be caring and attentive is met). And another thing: there's *never* enough stuff. Let me pause and say that this insightful psychological analysis is a result of my time at Frostburg State University in western Maryland where I majored in Psychology with a minor in Sledding on a Smuggled Cafeteria Tray. Everyone should visit Frostburg at least once during the winter. The snow usually melts in time for May's graduation ceremony.

Anyway, back to the collecting thing. Sometime around our transition from elementary school to junior high, Mom started collecting ceramic mice. She had them for every occasion. She had flag-waving mice for July 4th, Halloween mice peeking out of Jack-o-Lanterns, and Thanksgiving mice riding turkeys. But her favorites were the Christmas mice. They were everywhere and there were twice as many Christmas mice as any other kind. She had Santa Claus mice, mice pulling Santa's sleigh, Ebenezer Scrooge mice, mice holding candy canes, ice skating mice, caroling mice, mice on sleds (wearing little Frostburg State sweatshirts), shepherd mice, angel mice, and three wise mice on camels looking for Baby Jesus. It was insane! My father hated them but did his best to control his anger. He was not prone to profanity but did get upset from time to time, saying things like, "Those darn mice annoy the heck out of me," and "This whole mice thing is a bunch of bovine excrement." We lived in the country outside of Bel Air, Maryland, and our neighbors had a farm. So all of us were quite familiar with "bovine excrement." Plus, Dad worked for the federal government at Edgewood Arsenal where "bovine excrement" was continually produced—without cattle!

One Christmas season Mom put out all of her mice stuff. It was on the tables, on the mantel, and on the Christmas tree! I could never understand this because one time our cat caught a *real* mouse and deposited it on the front porch. Mom saw it and went nuts! She screamed and ran out the back door—terrified. So this whole obsession with ceramic mice never made sense to me. Mom loved them, though, so the men in the house had to put up with an army of ceramic mice.

We had a real tree that Christmas—a Scotch pine that Dad bought in Bel Air. Dad left it outside in a bucket of water until we were ready to decorate it. Then he brought this seven-and-a-half foot tree inside one night and set it up in the tree stand. It was BIG and smelled great! We put on the lights and ornaments, but only Mom could put on the mouse ornaments. *Lots* of them all over the tree, the tree which had been outside for a week. The same tree that provided shelter for birds and…you guessed it…a real *live* mouse! Yep, a real genuine mouse. Nothing ceramic about this vermin. He was the real deal. All he wanted was a warm and dry place to sleep, especially after the weather turned cold and snowy just prior to Christmas. So when Dad pulled the tree out of the bucket and brought it indoors, Mr. Mouse came along for the ride. He wasn't about to give up his new home in the Christmas tree, especially after it was moved into our nice warm house.

I guess the mouse wondered what was going on as he watched us from his place of concealment. He had to be confused by all of the ceramic mice hanging around him. I mean, they had to seem pretty unfriendly. They never responded when he said, "Merry Christmas!" or offered them eggnog. It had to be a lonely neighborhood in there so it was only a matter of time until the mouse ventured out.

Tramp was the first one to detect the mouse and this was not surprising since he was the ever-vigilant canine. He really should have ignored the mouse—for his own good. But vigilance and intelligence are not the same thing, as proven by Tramp. He majored in Vigilance with a minor in Stupid!

Tramp was on a probationary trial period because Mom did not allow animals inside the house—ever! The *only* reason the dog was allowed inside now was due to a severe cold spell with temperatures around zero overnight. Dad, B.G. and I convinced Mom that Tramp needed to be inside before he became a frozen *pupsicle.*

Tramp had to be on his best behavior to remain inside, but the presence of a mouse in the Christmas tree was just too much for any dog. I really believe the mouse was teasing Tramp and daring him to make a move. "Hey, Flea Motel, why don't you come and get me? Afraid you'll be put outside? C'mon mutt, who's your daddy?" That's what I think the mouse was trying to communicate to Tramp. There was a period of time when a stand-off existed between mouse and dog. Everybody was being cool and getting along. B.G. and I were doing the same thing. No need to jeopardize access to all those presents, at least not until the last one was opened. Then the free-for-all could begin. So we all behaved…and waited...B.G. and I, along with Tramp and the mouse. Everybody staying cool and staying under Mom's radar…until Christmas morning. Then things got a little crazy.

We had opened all of our presents and everyone was in the Christmas spirit. Even Tramp had a new chew toy so he was happy too. *Enter the mouse*! Now, I don't know if he got upset because he had no presents, or perhaps he was angry since he had no lady mouse to spend time with on Christmas day. Maybe we made too much noise and woke him up too early. Maybe he was a Jewish mouse or a Muslim mouse. Whatever the reason, the mouse went berserk! He climbed to the top of the tree and started gnawing on the star. Mom asked, "What's that noise?" Tramp started to growl and then he began to bark and lunged toward the tree. "What's the matter with that stupid dog?" yelled Dad. B.G. and I saw that Tramp's eyes were fixed on the top of the tree so we looked there. And we saw (and I'm not making this up) a mouse making a rude hand (paw?) gesture in Tramp's direction. "It's a mouse, it's a mouse!"

screamed B.G. "Of course it is," said Dad, "those darn things are everywhere!" I pointed to the top of the tree. "No, Dad, it's a *real* one!" This was when Mom started screaming hysterically. Dad took one of his new bedroom slippers (with a bright red bow still attached) and threw it at the mouse. The mouse jumped over to the mantel as the slipper shattered the star. Tramp (always slightly behind the action by a couple of seconds) saw the slipper falling from the tree and pounced on it. The slipper wasn't as good as catching a mouse, but it was better than a chew toy. Dad jumped up and said, "Faithful canine companion, I would prefer that you *not* chew on my slipper but instead return it to me forthwith, unscathed and minus slobbery dog drool." No, actually he said something like, "Give me that *now* you (expletive deleted) dog or you're dead meat!" Tramp jumped sideways to avoid Dad's grasp and knocked over the Christmas tree in the process. Mouse ornaments went everywhere!

My dad was a quick thinker and he took full advantage of the moment. "Honey, there's mice *everywhere*!" Now technically, this was *not* a lie. There were *ceramic* mice everywhere. But to my hysterical mother, they just had to be real *live* mice—invading our home and endangering our safety. "Kill them, kill them all!" screamed Mom as she climbed up on a chair…the chair beside the mantel. I swear that I saw, if just for one brief moment, a devilish grin on Dad's face. "Don't worry, my dear, I'll save you and the boys," said Dad as he began whacking the daylights out of those ceramic mice (with my brand-new Louisville Slugger baseball bat). It had to be one of the happiest moments of Dad's life. He got to destroy those hated ceramic mice…with Mom's encouragement! "Kill them, kill them all!" WHAM! "There's another one behind you!" WHAM! "Aieee, they're everywhere!" WHAM! WHAM! WHAM!

While Dad joyfully smashed ceramic mice, I watched the real mouse. He was a clever one, I'll tell you. He crept along the mantel until he arrived at the ceramic manger scene, then slipped inside and took the place of Baby Jesus. He even put up a little sign that read, "Wanted: Gold, Frankincense, and Muenster." He couldn't fool me, though, since his mouse ears and tail gave him away. This vermin really had some nerve! "There he is!" I yelled as loud as I could.

Now B.G. had loaded some ammo into his new Red Ryder BB gun as soon as he unwrapped it. In the time it took for all of this chaos to develop, B.G. had invented and mounted a laser sight on the BB gun. Mr. Mouse now had a bright red dot shining on his furry little chest and (I'm not making this up) he began to pray. B.G. later told me that the mouse also asked one of the ceramic mice (on a camel) for a blindfold. Anyway, B.G. was ready to make the mouse *permanently* go "away in the manger." Mom was totally on the verge of a psychotic break. Tramp was fixated on eating Dad's bedroom slipper, while Dad was obsessed with smashing all the ceramic mice into dust. So it was all up to B.G. and me to "save the day." Mom did not realize that the mouse was in the manger but assumed that it (and all its furry friends) were being destroyed by Dad. So when she saw B.G. aiming the BB gun at the manger she screamed, "What are you doing? Are you nuts? You're going to shoot Baby Jesus!"

B.G. tried to explain that the mouse was in the manger but Mom just screamed even louder, "Your father is killing the mouse over *there*!" B.G. ignored her as his finger tightened on the trigger, while the mouse asked another of the camel-riding mice for a last cigarette. "Please don't shoot Baby Jesus!" wailed Mom.

Now let's just pause for a moment here. Do you think, based on all you've read so far, that I was going to let this moment pass me by? My time had finally arrived to "settle the score" with B.G. Read on!

I grabbed a piece of paper and quickly drew a pentagram with the number 666 inside it. I stuck this to the back of B.G.'s pajama top with Silly Putty, looked at Mom, and yelled as loud as I possibly could, "NOW YOU KNOW!" Tramp stopped chewing. Dad, breathless but elated, stopped smashing. B.G.'s trigger finger relaxed. Mom, still standing on the chair, steadied herself by holding onto the mantel. In a low voice she whispered, "Know *what*?" I pointed to the manger and replied, "Who would dare to shoot Baby Jesus? *No one…*but the ANTI-CHRIST!!!" And I spun B.G. around 180 degrees so Mom could see the pentagram. "Aieee! Oh no, please no!" This was Mom's loudest scream yet, and it frightened the mouse so much that he bolted out of the manger and ran up inside the sleeve of Mom's robe. The poor woman was already "on the edge" after learning that her youngest child was the seed of Satan. A mouse running up her arm inside the robe was just too much, and I believe I'm recalling the incident correctly when I say that Mom fainted at this point.

Her last loud scream (prior to fainting and falling off the chair) so frightened B.G. (who now had the BB gun pointed at *Dad*) that he squeezed off a shot. OK, you figure it out. Red dot from a laser sight. Large man with a large butt. Dot on butt. BB follows dot at high velocity. Impact! Pain! Yelling! Words uttered which were totally inappropriate for Christmas Day. BB gun taken away from B.G. and crying by B.G. as he's banished to his room. Mom revived by Tramp licking her face. Mouse and I laugh until we cry!

Merry Christmouse, indeed! Bah, humbug!

PLAY BALL

As B.G. and I got older we became avid sports fans. We no longer lived in Baltimore but we were still die-hard supporters of the Orioles and the Colts. We had a real treat one summer day when Dad announced that he was taking us to an Orioles game! Ah, Memorial Stadium on 33rd St. It was a shrine, a temple…I mean, the Orioles and the Colts played there! So off we went on a fine summer day wearing Orioles caps and big smiles. Actually, B.G. had a huge grin on his face so I knew he was up to something.

We found our seats on the third base side of the field. Dad could not afford such great seats but one of the "big shots" where he worked (Edgewood Arsenal) gave him the tickets. The seats were ideal because they allowed us to be close to #5 (the greatest third baseman ever!), Brooks Robinson. We couldn't wait for the Orioles to take the field! And when they did, the loudest cheers were reserved for #5. And why not? "Brooksie" was a hero in Baltimore. He was like a vacuum cleaner at third base, gobbling up every ball that came in his direction. He made diving catches that were impossible for mortal men. Brooks Robinson was the best!

Now B.G. was determined to get Brooks' autograph. This, of course, required the invention of some device to make the task easier. When B.G. pulled this thing out from under his jacket and told me his plan, I then realized what his big grin was all about. He had taken a sling shot and modified it into something that resembled a crossbow with super space-age rubber. This thing could probably launch any projectile from Memorial Stadium all the way down to the harbor! B.G.'s "projectile" was a baseball with a pen taped to it. He planned to shoot the ball and pen onto the field near Brooks Robinson. In *theory*, Brooks would be so overwhelmed with B.G.'s devotion and ingenuity that he would autograph the ball and throw it back.

There was an important reality to be considered along with the theory. If a fan went onto the field or threw anything onto the field, said fan would be evicted from Memorial Stadium! B.G. knew this but I did not, so B.G. was able to "sucker" me quite easily. "You're my big brother and so much stronger than me. Why don't *you* shoot the ball and pen out there to Brooks? Boy, won't he be impressed with *you*!" (I still can't believe that I fell for this.)

We waited patiently for the right moment which was, of course, any moment when Dad happened to not be around. At the bottom of the third inning Dad announced, "Boys, I'm going to the restroom, but I'll be right back. Stay in your seats and *Behave!*" So Dad was off to the restroom and out came the slingshot/crossbow/eviction device. B.G. ceremoniously presented it to me with these words, "You're the best big brother any kid could ever have!" (I must have been the most *gullible* big brother in the world because B.G. never seemed to have any problem manipulating me.) I was almost tearful as I took the "deadly weapon" (this was the term used by the police later in the day, but I'll get to that soon) from a fawning B.G. The moment had arrived. I loaded the baseball and attached pen, aimed and fired, but things did not work out as planned.

Actually, things went downhill...real fast! The "beer guy" a few rows down ended up in the line of fire and barely avoided getting "beaned." The ball and pen passed right in front of his nose (at a *very* high rate of speed), resulting in a major beer spill. Pabst Blue Ribbon and National Bohemian went everywhere! Now, you have to understand something. Spilling beer in Baltimore is almost as serious as spilling communion wine at church! Hitting "beer guy" is almost as serious as hitting a priest! Anyway, the "deadly projectile" (this was another term used by the police, and I *promise* to explain) did not actually strike the "beer guy" but it did make him spill all the beer he was carrying. The projectile (still accelerating) continued onward toward the box seats down in front. About this time a guy in one of the box seats stood up and had his "flat top" haircut grazed ever so slightly by said projectile. Since he was in a front row box seat, the guy was obviously important or had money. Or both. This was a case of "both." This guy was the most famous owner of a "flat top" in Baltimore…Johnny Unitas! The quarterback for the Baltimore Colts was there watching the Orioles game and I nearly "beaned" him. "Johnny U." was as beloved in Baltimore as Brooks Robinson! I almost hit Johnny Unitas (and "beer guy")! Was I insane???

But wait, because this story isn't over. The ever-accelerating "projectile," after barely missing "beer guy" and Johnny Unitas, continued onward in its destructive endeavor. It was on a high-speed trajectory towards third base…and Brooks Robinson! Toward the *nose* of Brooks Robinson! At the last second, out of the corner of his eye, Brooks saw the ball and pen coming at him. He had the reflexes of a cat. Brooks brought his glove up and snagged the ball and attached pen just like he snagged hot line drives rocketing down the third base line! The crowd went wild!

Now pitcher Milt Pappas was in his wind-up and still had the official game ball in his glove. The umpire behind catcher Gus Triandos saw Brooks catch *my* ball and yelled, "Time out!" Shortstop Luis Aparicio came over to see if Brooks was OK, and then Brooks walked over to check on Johnny Unitas (who was looking up at "beer guy"). And "beer guy" was *very* busy apologizing to a very burly guy who was "out sick" from his job at Bethlehem Steel. Burly steelworker was covered in beer and quite upset (mainly because he was now on TV and didn't look too sick). Then EVERYONE started to look at me and B.G. No, wait…B.G. had disappeared! He had moved to a vacant seat three rows *behind* me while Brooks was checking on "Johnny U." I was all alone with my "deadly weapon" as B.G. yelled, "There he is, right there, that kid with the crossbow! He did it!" (What a little traitor!)

Dad returned about this time and asked, "Where's your little brother?" Before I could answer, Dad said, "You're the oldest and you have to watch out for him. Can't I even go pee without a problem here?" Dad knew nothing about what had just happened, but he was about to find out. The police arrived as an unruly mob formed around us. B.G. also arrived, hugged Dad and said, "I missed you, Father. I love you *so* much! But I fear that my older brother has taken advantage of your absence to engage in mischief." (I know it sounds weird but sometimes he talked like that.) Before I could say, "It was *your* idea!" a cop grabbed me by the arm. When Dad asked, "What's going on?" another cop grabbed Dad by the arm. The cop asked, "Is that your kid?" Dad thought for a moment and then replied, "It all depends. First tell me what he did."

So it all came out: slingshot/crossbow, "beer guy," Johnny U. and Brooks, attempted assault, attempted murder, use of a deadly weapon in the commission of a felony, etc., etc. Dad just stood there with his mouth open. He stared at me and his face got red. B.G. asked, "Dad, are you OK?" Dad looked at the cops and said, "Arrest me now before I commit some serious child abuse on this kid!" B.G. yelled, "Hey beer guy. Bring this man a frosty cold one and make it quick!" Beer guy could not comply because all his beer was spilled and he was also in handcuffs. The restraints were necessary because "beer guy" was going berserk and screaming, "I'm going to kill that kid with the crossbow!" People around us were going nuts! "You little delinquent, you tried to kill Johnny Unitas!" yelled one man. Another screamed, "You almost killed Brooks Robinson!" An old lady hollered, "Worst of all, you little hea-then, you made the beer guy spill my National Bo. You should be locked up!" B.G. looked at her and exclaimed, "Grandma, I didn't know you were here at the game."

Things were getting ugly. Chuck Thompson, the radio an-nouncer for the Orioles, told his audience that I was obviously a "troubled youth who listened to too much rock and roll." The police escorted us out of the stands for our own safety. One guy offered me $10 for the crossbow as the police dragged me by. He wanted it for the Colts-Jets football game in the fall so he could "give that punk Joe Namath an attitude adjustment."

Anyway, let's just say that I was the loser that day (along with the Orioles). And guess who the winner was...*again*? Yes, my younger brother. B.G. *did* get Brooks' autograph (and Johnny U.) because he (and let me quote the *Baltimore Sun* here) "showed remarkable courage by identifying the miscreant" (that was me, and I thought I was Presbyterian). The *Sun* continued, "Young Ronald (B.G.—if you have not been paying attention) prevented further endangerment of the public" and "The young hero saved our beloved Brooks Robinson and Johnny Unitas from certain injury and possible death." Oh, please! Who wrote the article...Harry Hyperbole?

I was "grounded" by Dad, fingerprinted by the Baltimore Police Department, vilified by the *Baltimore Sun* and WBAL-TV, and humiliated by B.G. And for my own safety, I was banned from Memorial Stadium for the rest of my life.

THE BEACH BOYS

One of the greatest musical groups of my generation was the Beach Boys. I loved their great harmonies on songs like "Help Me, Rhonda," "Surfer Girl," "Be True to Your School," and countless others. The only problem was that I (along with B.G.) had never actually seen the ocean or surfers, despite singing along with the Beach Boys whenever they were on the radio. B.G. and I developed an affinity for the ocean and beach life from listening to the Beach Boys, so it was only natural that we began to long for an actual encounter with the ocean. This finally occurred just as we hit our preteen years when friends invited our family to Ocean City, New Jersey.

I can tell you that B.G. and I were truly overwhelmed when we saw the Atlantic Ocean for the first time. It just seemed to go on forever; why, it was enormous! And those waves rolling in, one after another…crashing and foaming and receding…over and over again. We went nuts! It was one big wet playground just ideal for the two of us. And that is when my brother and I became the "beach boys" (*not* THE Beach Boys) because each of us fell in love with beach life at that time. My brother returns to Ocean City, New Jersey, each year to spend a week there at the beach and still loves it as much as he did during our childhood. I now live farther south and frequent North Myrtle Beach in South Carolina every chance I get. Let me tell you this: *Nothing* can "soothe the soul" like a week at the beach.

B.G. and I took to the ocean like we were born there. Both of us were competent swimmers and we quickly learned to bodysurf and ride the waves on rubber rafts. Mom and Dad never learned to swim so both of them were naturally fearful for us as well as for themselves. We were rarely able to coax Mom and Dad out beyond knee-deep water. B.G. and I went out as far as the lifeguards would allow, and this was never too far or too dangerous. The lifeguards in the Ocean City Beach

Patrol were always on the lookout for stupid kids like us and when they blew their whistles, we responded. These guys were professional and their word was "law" on the beach and in the surf. No one, even "tough guys," challenged the lifeguards. If they told you to move closer to shore or get out of the water, you did it. They took their job of protecting the public very seriously and we took their authority very seriously!

A couple of the lifeguards at the beach we regularly visited were just nice guys. Joe and Sam talked to our parents as if they were old friends, took B.G. and me out in the lifeboat for an exciting ride, and even let us sit with them in the lifeguard stand! We became their "mascots" and would go down to the beach in the mornings to help them bring down all their gear to the water's edge. This "work" entitled us to the above-mentioned privileges plus free use of the rubber rafts. One evening Joe took us on the boardwalk and we had free rides, pizza, and miniature golf. He knew everyone (or so it seemed) and "freebies" were readily available because he was a lifeguard! I mean, people almost worshipped these guys!

Don and Ron with Sam and Joe, lifeguards at Ocean City, NJ

It was a magical time, I tell you. We swam, walked on the beach, hung out with cool lifeguards, drooled over cute girls, and enjoyed *freedom* from Mom and Dad! Could life possibly get any better? You see, Mom was the original "Queen of Worry" and "Princess of Over-Protection." B.G. and I were on the verge of becoming teenagers and we needed some SPACE! Please!!! So any opportunity to have some freedom was more than welcome, and we took full advantage of it. Ocean City, New Jersey, was, at that time, one of the safest places in the world (my brother says that this is still the case). The lifeguards protected you on the beach and in the surf, and the police maintained a highly visible presence on the boardwalk. You rarely saw any drunks, fights, or rowdiness because it was just not tolerated there. No alcohol was sold on the island of Ocean City, New Jersey, and you still have to go across the bridge to the mainland to get booze even today. Our parents were absolute non-drinkers so the alcohol-free atmosphere at Ocean City really appealed to them. Founded by Methodists as a Christian seaside resort, Ocean City had the family environment that our parents preferred. This environment allowed our parents to "loosen the reins" a great deal on me and B.G. We had the opportunity to "stretch our wings" a little bit in a safe and fun place where even *we* could not get into too much trouble.

Well, maybe we could get into *some* trouble. I mean, it was me and B.G., right? We had reputations to uphold and peers to impress, parents to stress, and *each other* to annoy and harass as much as possible. So let me just be honest and say that perhaps there were a *few* times when the "beach boys" got into a little trouble.

Sometimes the trouble began even *before* we got to the beach. On one occasion, B.G. decided that our dog Tramp deserved a trip to the beach since he was part of the family. That's logical, isn't it? Maybe so, but the illogical part was smuggling Tramp into the *trunk* of the car for a three-hour ride to Ocean City! The only thing that saved the mutt was the fact that we had a flat tire somewhere near the Conowingo Dam. Dad had to pull onto the shoulder of Route 1 to change the tire and he was NOT a happy man. Opening the trunk to get the spare tire and jack saved the dog's life since it was ninety degrees outside and probably one hundred and fifty degrees inside the trunk! Again, B.G. could sure do some stupid stuff at times, despite his super I.Q. Anyway, Dad opened the trunk and got tackled by a panting pooch who expressed gratitude for being freed by giving Dad copious amounts of slobbery dog kisses. This did *not* improve Dad's mood at all. He yelled, "Get this mutt off of me!" just before he screamed, "Boys, get out of the car, NOW!" And here was the amazing part: B.G. actually admitted that *he* put Tramp in the trunk. I'm not sure if he was afraid of what Dad was going to do to him, or if he was feeling really guilty because he almost killed our dog via heat stroke.

Mom jumped out of the car to save B.G.'s life. She knew that Dad was ready to throw the brat off the dam and into the churning waters of the Susquehanna River far below. Tramp, still panting, trotted over to a roadside puddle for a drink of much-needed water before peeing all over the flat tire that Dad was preparing to change. Things were pretty tense until a pickup truck stopped behind us. It was Dominic and his uncle on their way to the dam for a fishing trip. They helped Dad change the tire and agreed to take Tramp with them for the day and then return him to Thelma Lou's house (she was dog-sitting while we went to the beach). We then proceeded on our way and B.G. didn't say a word until somewhere near Somers Point or May's Landing. Dad frequently glared at him in the rearview mirror while muttering threats under his breath. Mom patted Dad on the arm and repeatedly said, "Be calm, Dear, just be calm." I suggested that we put B.G. in the trunk for the remainder of the trip so he could comprehend how poor Tramp must have felt. Dad and B.G. both glared at me prior to Mom stating, "If you don't shut up right now I will make your father turn this car around and go back home!" It was a "Mom-ism" but I really thought she was serious on this occasion. It was a *very* quiet trip from that point, but we did get to the beach.

It was really funny to see B.G. get ready for the beach trip. The kid just went nutso! We usually made the trip during the first week of August but B.G. started packing around Easter. He crossed the days off on his calendar, and every night at supper he would announce, "Only one hundred days until beach time!"…"Only ninety nine days until beach time!" (You get the idea.) This went on night after night. When school ended in early June we were allowed to stay up later, but B.G. would go to bed even *earlier*, announcing to the family that he had to "get rested up for the beach trip." I mean, it was insane! The kid just lived for that beach vacation.

The night before the trip was chaotic! I shared a bedroom with B.G. and had to put up with his last minute pre-trip preparations. He insisted on blowing up the rubber raft at this time and, of course, we had no air pump. Have you ever tried to inflate one of those things with just lung power? It was exhausting! B.G. also insisted on wearing his bathing suit and swim fins to bed and this would have been fine except for the fact that we shared the bed. Ever try to sleep with swim fins smacking you in the face and/or crotch all night long?

On the morning of another trip B.G. showed up at the breakfast table with the aforementioned bathing suit and swim fins, plus his snorkel and swim mask. Mom allowed the suit and fins but "drew the line" at the mask and snorkel. B.G. protested, but Mom replied, "You can't eat your breakfast with the mask and snorkel on, and we will *not* leave this house without breakfast!" End of discussion! B.G. quickly complied, breakfast was consumed, and off we went (but only after Dad checked the trunk for stowaway canines). Now B.G. was exhausted from staying up most of the previous night to inflate the rubber raft so he fell asleep early into the trip. He was still wearing his bathing suit (called "swimming trunks" in those days) and swim fins. He also had on his swim mask (not on top of his head but over his face) and the snorkel between his lips. As a result, he could not breathe through his nose but only through the snorkel tube in his mouth. This was just too tempting for me. I made sure that Mom and Dad weren't looking and then I dropped a Cheerio down into the top of the snorkel opening. Down it went! B.G. quickly sucked it in, choked, and coughed it out of his mouth and back up through the tube. Blast off! I picked it off of the ceiling of our Chevy Impala and dropped it back into the snorkel tube. Inhale, choke, cough, blast off, retrieve from ceiling of auto…and repeat the cycle. I amused myself for miles like this until Mom turned around and asked, "Ronald, are you all right, dear?" (I feigned sleep at this point.) B.G. stirred briefly, mumbled that he was OK (perhaps he said, "Please help me because I think my brother is trying to kill me while I sleep"), and then he fell back to sleep. I opened one eye just enough to see if B.G. was back in Dream Land and Mom was no longer watching him. All clear! Then I decided it was time to kick things up a notch. I quietly reached over toward B.G. and plugged the snorkel with my thumb. After a few seconds the brat started to gasp for air while flailing his arms and legs. It was a riot! I removed my thumb before he attracted Mom's attention or woke up. Then I waited a few minutes until he calmed down and settled back into a deep sleep. Hey, that was fun! Let's do it *again*! And I did…repeatedly. The biggest problem was trying to contain my laughter. I mean, this was some great amusement and a wonderful way to pass the time during a boring trip. B.G. was like a little wind-up toy that I could abuse all the way from Bel Air, Maryland, to Ocean City, New Jersey! When he starting flailing his arms and legs he reminded me of that robot from the "Lost in Space" TV show ("Warning, Will Robinson, warning!").

I finally went too far and B.G. woke up while gasping for air. He ripped off his mask and snorkel and began to cry, telling Mom that he had a bad dream about being attacked by some evil Cheerios. Mom told Dad to pull the car over so she could get out and check on "poor little Ronald" (the little whiney cry-baby). Dad asked me if I knew what was going on, so I told him that B.G. obviously suffered from Sleep Apnea! I sure enjoyed that trip!

B.G. couldn't wait to get into the water when we arrived in Ocean City. He annoyed Dad and Mom (and me) as the car was being unloaded at our little cottage. He continued to wear his mask, fins, and snorkel while he ran around yelling, "Let's go to the beach! Let's go swimming!" All of this activity created lots of perspiration, and eventually B.G.'s mask would fog up. Would he take it off so the inside of the mask could clear? Heck, no! B.G. wasn't about to take off that mask, snorkel, or fins because he had to be *ready* when Dad gave us the "green light" to go swimming. I did not want him to remove the mask because it was so amusing to watch him run into things (fire hydrants, telephone poles, the car) because the fog inside the mask obscured his vision. I would even tell him, "Whatever you do, *don't* take off your mask. You want to be ready to go when Dad and Mom take us to the beach!" I also said things like, "Girls really think that guys in swim masks are cool!" or "You almost look like a manly lifeguard with that mask on!" He actually believed this stuff!!! I had to ask myself at times if this kid could really have an I.Q. of 210. I mean, can you be that dumb if you are really that smart?

B.G. would eventually run into something and get hurt, start crying, be consoled by Mom, and then told by Dad to "just get out of the way and go invent something." Whoa, Pops! Bad move by the old Paternal Unit! That was the *last* thing you ever wanted to say to B.G. He was prone to invent, create, and "tweak" even without encouragement, so what do you think he was capable of when told to "go invent something"? I mean, this little evil genius was dangerous enough when we tried to *restrain* those creative juices! Now my poor unsuspecting father had "unleashed the beast" upon the quiet little beachside town of Ocean City, New Jersey.

B.G. went into the storage shed behind our little cottage and began to create. The rest of us were just glad to have some peace and quiet as we unpacked the car and moved into our cottage. We heard nothing from B.G. for quite awhile. He finally reappeared when Mom announced that lunch was ready. We ate and then (drum roll, please) *finally* headed down to the beach for an afternoon of sun, sand, and surf. It was a long walk to the beach, but Dad told us that there was no use to take the car and then have no place to park. It was a hot Saturday and Ocean City was packed with "weekenders." Parking spaces were scarce, indeed, and Dad knew better than to load everything into the car and then drive around for forty-five minutes trying to find a place to park. When I protested about the long walk Dad replied, "Stop complaining, boy! Why, when I was in the Army during WW II we had to march for miles everyday while dodging bullets!" In a moment of temporary insanity, I countered with, "Yeah, and I bet you had to walk to and from school through eight feet of snow uphill both ways after milking the cows by hand before dawn in sub-zero temperatures!" Now the minute that little retort was out of my mouth I knew I was in trouble. (But it was a pretty good comeback, don't you think?) Dad smacked me in the back of the head so fast that I had no time to duck (he was big, and he was fast!), and YES, I saw stars. No one in those days ever talked about "child abuse." Smart-mouthed kids got smacked or spanked (or both) all the time. The little heathens never called Social Services or Child Protective Services or whatever because they knew they *deserved* to get whacked! And I deserved this little dose of fatherly discipline because I had "smarted off" to my Dad…in front of other adults! (Which made it a *public* offense rather than a private one, and therefore more heinous.) Indeed, some other adults on the street saw this and said things like: "Give that smart-mouthed brat another smack!" and "If that was my kid he'd be out cold by now!" and "Good job, Mister. America needs more fathers like you!" If any adult had stuck his/her nose into Dad's business and told Dad to stop "abusing" me or Social Services would be contacted, Dad (and anyone else nearby) would have called that person a "Pinko Commie" who needed to mind his/her own business or get hurt. Yeah, baby…Can't you just feel the love?

I quickly apologized to Dad and all was forgiven. That was my Dad. When it was over, it was over! And I knew that later *he* would apologize to *me* for losing his temper. Punishment was swift and sure, reconciliation occurred, and then we went on with life. And I learned a valuable lesson about respect. I didn't really need to look to the lifeguards or Mickey Mantle or Johnny Unitas for a hero. I lived with one everyday!

B.G. loved it when Dad "nailed" me and he laughed at me block after block. In between bouts of laughter B.G. kept adjusting the large load in the wagon behind him. He had discovered the wagon in the shed behind the cottage last summer, and our landlady said we could use it to transport stuff to the beach. This was B.G.'s job each summer at the beach, and he loved the challenge of packing and securing all of our junk (cooler, rubber raft, beach chairs, towels, etc.). He did such a great job that Mom and Dad just turned the responsibility over to him and never even looked in the wagon. B.G. never forgot anything and never had any of the junk fall off the wagon. He also attached a small solar-powered motor (Yes, he was a pioneer in this field) so the wagon was self-propelled. All B.G. had to do was steer it. But it seemed to me that the wagon's load was larger than usual this time so I tried to peek under the tarp covering the load (we used the tarp for shade). B.G. quickly protested, and Mom reminded me that "Ronald takes care of the wagon," so I backed off without checking the contents. Still, something was amiss.

When we arrived at the beach and found a spot to "set up camp," B.G. told Mom and Dad, "It was a long, hot walk. Why don't you two go cool off in the water while I unpack the wagon?" The Parental Units quickly bought into this idea and went on into the surf, but I was suspicious. And why not? B.G. had been wearing his bathing suit, swim fins, mask and snorkel for *months*! Remember, this was the kid who was so anxious to get into the water that he almost needed to be restrained in a straitjacket and pumped full of heavy-duty medication! And now he was going to resist the "siren song of the surf?" (I made that up and it sounded good so I had to use it. Don't you just love the alliteration?) Anyway, I knew that B.G. was up to something so I watched him closely. He tried to get me to go down to the water but I refused, so B.G. said, "You have to promise to keep this a secret." He then pulled back a corner of the tarp to reveal a *mechanical shark*! Before I could say anything B.G. told me, "I have good news and bad news. The good news is that this thing is remote-controlled. The bad news is that your Robert the Robot has been sacrificed for the good of science." I advanced toward B.G. with the intent of bodily harm, but he countered with, "Wait, wait, I'll let you operate it first. Just don't tell Mom and Dad."

So once again I got "sucked in" on a B.G. scheme, foolishly helping him drag the tarp-covered mechanical shark out into the surf. A couple of people looked at us suspiciously, but we just kept on going until we could slip the shark into the water. B.G. held onto it while I took the tarp back to our site and encountered Mom and Dad. All they said was, "You boys be careful and don't go out too far." Then it was naptime for them. Lights out. Sleep peacefully. Don't worry about your two little angels preparing to create a major *panic* on a crowded New Jersey beach on a Saturday afternoon in August during the height of the tourist season! I returned to B.G. and the shark. The surf was not overly rough so B.G. had no trouble holding onto Mr. Shark, especially since it was perfectly counter-weighted to ride low in the water with only the large dorsal fin visible. But wait! Where was the dorsal fin? B.G. told me that the presence of the dorsal fin sticking up in the air would have been a dead giveaway, so he concealed it inside the body of the shark. The remote control unit had a switch to raise and lower the fin on command! WOW! This kid was GOOD! Also, the shark was not at full length because B.G. designed it to fit onto the wagon for ease of concealment. The shark had a body that would expand lengthwise (in telescope fashion) when activated from the remote control unit. So Mr. Shark would eventually grow from his current length of three feet to an intimidating dimension of ten feet! Now doesn't the thought of this thing in the water with you bring out the urge to go swimming?

B.G. had me hold onto the shark while he ran back to our "command center" on the beach. Mom and Dad were sound asleep so B.G. had no trouble removing the remote control unit from the wagon. He raised the antenna and activated the shark's expansion switch, waving at me to release the creature. It was pretty impressive to watch the shark expand to its full ten-foot length just under the surface of the water, and then slowly swim out into deeper water as B.G. activated more controls. I ran in towards the shore to join B.G. and become a certified "shark driver." "Remember your promise," I told him, "you said I could operate it first." B.G. hesitated, so I said, "I'm sure there was something I needed to tell Mom and Dad." That did it! Nothing like a little blackmail to get your own way! So B.G. reluctantly handed me the remote control unit and proceeded to lecture me on how to operate it. "Whatever you do, don't hit *that* switch!" I asked why, and B.G. explained that it was the switch that raised the dorsal fin. "You don't want to raise the fin too close to all the swimmers. They'll go crazy and think that it's a *real* shark!"

Now, excuse me for a moment. I thought the whole idea was to make this thing look like a real shark! I mean, why did it have an expandable body and a dorsal fin which could rise up out of the shark's body? What was the point in keeping the dorsal fin concealed and letting the shark swim around unde-tected just under the surface of the water? No one, except me and B.G., would even know that the thing was out there. But my brother was adamant. "I mean it! Don't raise the dorsal fin! You'll have a mass panic if people think there's a real shark in the water!" I asked why he even bothered to create the shark if it was to be concealed during its entire "maiden voyage." B.G.'s reply, "I just wanted to see if I could build it and if it would actually work. Plus, I have a possible contract pending with the U.S. Navy for some Top Secret work if the shark checks out OK. I could tell you more about that but then I'd have to kill you."

Oh, well pardon me, Mr. Government Contractor for the Military-Industrial Complex! Don't let a little day of fun at the beach during our ONLY week of vacation at Ocean City get in the way of *your* career! B.G. knew I was upset so he walked away to let me cool down, reminding me again to NOT raise the dorsal fin. He headed up to the boardwalk for a slice of Mack and Manco's pizza, leaving me to operate Mr. Shark all by myself. I heeded his warning (it was his shark, after all) and continued to drive the shark into deeper water as I tracked it by the small wake it created (since I could not track it by the dorsal fin). Eventually the shark got out so far that I could not see the wake. I panicked! I had absolutely *no* idea where the creature was, and I began to punch buttons and hit switches recklessly. (Must find shark! Must find shark!) Just try to guess which switch I accidentally hit during my panic attack. Think hard! Remember B.G.'s warning.

Oh yeah, baby! I hit the Forbidden Switch! What a naughty boy! That's right; I flipped the old Dorsal Fin Activation Switch and up came the dorsal fin to a height of about three feet! B.G. had warned me *not* to do so, but it was an accident! I didn't mean to do it…it just happened. Suddenly both of the lifeguards in the guard stand stood up and one focused his binoculars offshore. They briefly conferred and then the other guard climbed on *top* of the guard stand to increase his visibility to everyone out in the water. He began to blow his whistle frantically while motioning for the swimmers to get out of the water NOW! Several people on shore stopped broiling in the sun long enough to stand up and look out into the water, and suddenly one fat guy yelled, "SHARK!!!" He was pointing out to a location just beyond the swimmers and I focused my attention there. And lo and behold, *there* was Mr. Shark swimming rapidly toward the beach and a few hundred unsuspecting bathers. "There you are, you cute little rascal," I said aloud. His dorsal fin was knifing through the water at full speed and, I tell you, it was a thing of beauty. B.G. had really done a great job this time. The shark looked and swam just like a real one and I just stood there on the beach enjoying the sight. Boy, did that thing look real! WAIT! That's the problem, moron! Focus, focus. Find the right control and drop the dorsal fin while turning the shark away from shore. NO, not that one! That only increased the shark's speed and made him open his mouth wide, showing all those TEETH! Idiot! Oh heck, just start punching buttons and flipping switches because the shark was now totally *out of control* and had gone into Attack Mode! ("It's alive, it's alive!") The shark now seemed to have a mind of its own and failed to respond to any button or switch that I hit. (B.G. later told me that my panic switching had short-circuited the creature and rendered the remote control unit absolutely useless.)

Well, you can imagine what happened next. It was one of the worst stampedes in the history of mankind! People started screaming, "SHARK!" at the top of their lungs as they trampled one another while trying to get out of the water. Children were crying hysterically as their parents scooped them up and ran for shore. Rubber rafts were left bobbing in the water as people jumped off and struggled to get away from the "killer shark." I saw people get knocked down and trampled as panic swept the beach. Several people fainted and one elderly man complained of chest pains. The lifeguards had their hands full trying to get everyone out of the water and then tend to the injured. Two police officers ran down from the boardwalk to help out along with lifeguards from the adjoining beaches. B.G. returned about this time with a piece of pepperoni hanging from his lower lip. He took one look at me and said, "You're an idiot, did you know that? A moron who's lucky to even get a 'D minus' in school! I told you *not* to raise the dorsal fin. Now look what you've done!" He started running down to the water, stopped, then turned back toward me. "Take a long last look at the ocean, Bro, 'cause you're headed off to Reform School for sure this time!" He then continued on to the water's edge to help the injured. (Did I mention that B.G. was a certified paramedic and had already been accepted into Johns Hopkins medical school?) I decided that I should help someone so I picked…ME! Yeah, before this was over I was going to need some serious help. The first order of business to help myself was to get rid of the evidence, so I found a kid's sand shovel and quickly buried the remote control unit. No need to get caught with that! Maybe I was a consistent "D minus" student, but I knew how to cover my backside when trouble was brewing. I looked toward the water and saw B.G. headed into the waves with a surfboard! People were yelling, screaming, and crying. The lifeguards and cops tried to stop B.G., but he was too fast. "Come back, you crazy kid. It's suicide if you go out there. That shark will rip you to pieces!"

Now my brother always had a plan and this time was no exception. After helping the injured, splinting two broken legs, and delivering a baby (an emergency seaside C-section), he was off to take care of the shark. A surfboard was all he needed to get out into the water and deal with the rampaging shark. B.G. was in minimal danger because he (and I) knew that the shark was not real; but remember, no one else knew this. People on shore thought that he was either crazy or very brave, but B.G. was just being his usual over-achieving self. Suddenly one woman screamed, "My daughter, she's still out there!" and everyone looked out beyond Surfer Boy (B.G.) to see a beautiful teenage girl on a rubber raft being circled by a ravenous (or so it seemed) ten-foot shark! The beast was running out of juice from its power unit (B.G. had yet to perfect Plutonium as a power source) as it swam in circles. Each circuit around the girl brought the shark closer and closer to her, and it appeared to the girl and everyone on shore that the shark was closing in for the kill! Actually, Mr. Shark was just about out of power and only capable of swimming feebly in ever-decreasing circles. The young girl just happened to be in the middle of the circles and thought that she was facing certain death. She was screaming and crying as the shark drew closer. Her mother fainted and people cried and yelled on shore while watching to see what B.G. was going to do. It was a tense moment, and I also wondered just what B.G. had planned.

Surfer Boy paddled up to the now-hysterical girl just as the shark bumped against her raft and knocked her into the water. She screamed and swallowed lots of water while everyone on the beach yelled, "Oh no, she's gone!" and "The shark got her!" and "That crazy kid on the surfboard is next!" But B.G. was the "Man of the Hour" as he grabbed the girl and pulled her up onto the surfboard. Everyone stopped crying and began to cheer wildly but one of the lifeguards said, "They still have to get away from that big shark." Well, not really. The shark was, by now, out of juice and essentially "dead." No one but B.G. realized this, and even the girl on the surfboard with him had fainted and never realized that the shark was a fake. B.G. paddled in furiously, caught a wave, stood up while holding the unconscious beauty in his arms, and "hung ten" like a pro. He rode the wave all the way to shore as the crowd went absolutely crazy. TV crews had arrived and they filmed the rescue by B.G., and also captured his proudest moment when he gave the girl mouth-to-mouth resuscitation. Some guys just get all the breaks, don't they? I mean, this girl was gorgeous and looked like a model (I think her name was Farrah or something like that) and here was B.G. with his lips on hers! Is there no justice? Would B.G. have had the opportunity to rescue this babe and "make out" with her (no one does mouth-to-mouth for twenty minutes, especially *after* the person resumes breathing!) if not for me? This kid just continued to "kick my butt" every chance he got. He helped the now-revived beauty to her feet and got a big hug and a very passionate kiss from her (Yeah, it made the 6:00 PM national news) as well as a hug from her mother. People were cheering and clapping while girls ran up to B.G. to kiss him and drop off their phone numbers. The cops and lifeguards shook hands with B.G. and congratulated him, while the mayor of Ocean City arrived to give my brother the key to the city and a guarantee of a free lifetime supply of Mack and Manco's pizza. He was their hero and still is, because even today he cannot walk down the boardwalk without people asking him for his autograph. But a hero's work is never done, as proven by B.G.'s next move.

B.G. said, "Excuse me folks, but there's still a dangerous shark lurking out there and waiting to gobble up one of your beloved children." (Oh please, give me a break! It was a fake shark with a dead battery. It was about as dangerous as my Robert the Robot, and actually contained some of old Robert's hardware.) B.G. grabbed the surfboard and then grabbed the "babe," kissed her passionately and said, "If I don't come back, always remember this moment!" Then he was off to the surf and the shark while people said things like, "He has to be the bravest kid on the planet!" and "He's sooooo cute!" and "There goes a true American hero!" and...well, you get the picture. I thought I was going to puke! This little over-achiever was going to "milk" this situation for all it was worth! He knew that the shark was a fake (and a dead fake, at that) but he was determined to enhance his hero status even more. I was hoping that he would drown or be attacked by a real shark! B.G. paddled out to the shark and everyone on shore gasped, but, of course, they still thought the shark was real. He tapped the shark on its snout and it suddenly reared up out of the water. (B.G. later told me that static electricity from his touch briefly energized the beast.) Everyone on shore gasped again as the shark began to tail-walk across the waves and gyrate like it was disco dancing or doing the Macarena (neither of which had been "invented" yet). Years later I thought about this incident during the disco craze and decided that if the shark had been dressed in polyester it could have been mistaken for John Travolta in *Saturday Night Fever*. B.G. then jumped from the surfboard onto the *back* of the shark and rode it around rodeo-style while people on shore just stared in disbelief. He then used some wrasslin' moves (that's *wrestling,* for those of you who are ignorant of America's greatest sport) on Mr. Shark. In the space of about two minutes I saw B.G. do a Suplex, the Figure 4 Leg Vine, the Sleeper Hold, and a Flying Drop Kick on that shark! If the thing had not been dead already, B.G. would surely have killed it with his wrestling repertoire! It was an awesome display of wrestling skills, or at least that was what Johnny Valentine, Bruno Sanmartino, Haystacks Calhoun, and Nature Boy Rick Flair said about it on the news that night. The crowd screamed, yelled, and cheered as their hero sent the shark to the bottom of the ocean. The evil man-eater was dead and gone, and Ocean City, New Jersey, could once again return to its peaceful existence as a happy beachside town. B.G. surfed back in and was kissed by girls, given generous slices of pizza, applauded and interviewed, and then hoisted onto the shoulders of his admirers for a victory ride down the boardwalk. Mom and Dad woke from their nap about this time and asked, "Where's your brother?" as well as "What's going on?" and finally "What did you do *this* time?" Before I could answer some guys in Navy uniforms walked up to Dad, whispered something in his ear, and handed him a check with *lots* of zeroes. I just walked away shaking my head and muttering to myself.

Suddenly a kid walked up to me and asked, "Can we talk for a minute?" I had no desire to deal with any of B.G.'s worshippers so I turned and walked away. The kid persisted and then his father arrived to join in the conversation. "Look here," the father said, "we saw what happened and we know that you were operating that fake shark by remote control." He then pulled a sandy remote control unit out of his beach bag. I panicked! Before I could say anything, the kid's father said, "Hey, relax. We're not going to tell anyone. We just want that shark. I'm going to go out with scuba gear when things quiet down and retrieve it." I explained that the Navy had already stopped by to see Dad and drop off a large check, and I then pointed out toward the shark's last-known location. "Oh no!" said the father. He was upset because Navy divers were already jumping into the water from a small boat to get the shark. I said, "Sorry, it would have been OK with me if you got the shark because I don't need any more evidence showing up." The kid laughed and replied, "Yeah, and no one needs to know that your brother is *not* the big hero of Ocean City. Man, what a hot dog!" The kid's father was quiet for a minute and then asked, "Do you think that you could find your brother's design plans for the shark? I really need them!" I explained that my brother was the Boy Genius and the plans were all in his *head*. He never needed to write anything down because he had total recall, a photographic memory, etc. I then asked the father why he wanted the shark so badly, and he told me this (and it's the truth): "My name is Spielberg and this is my son, Stevie. He hopes to be a famous movie producer one day, and he feels that today's events would make a great movie. Imagine a movie about a large shark terrorizing a small beach-side town! It could be a box office bonanza!" I laughed so hard that tears came to my eyes. "You've got to be kidding!" I

The "beach boys" Don and Ron, August 1963

77

said between fits of laughter, "Who in their right mind would want to see a movie like that?" Little Stevie and Mr. Spielberg shrugged their shoulders and walked away. I never saw or heard from them again, and I have no idea what became of Little Stevie, the budding director. I hope the kid grew up and got a real job because he obviously was not movie director material. I mean, how stupid can you get? A movie about a shark attacking people at the beach—why, that's as stupid as a movie about encounters with aliens or some other wacky stuff! I felt sorry for Little Stevie, I really did, because the kid was going nowhere. What a loser!

Anyway, back to B.G. and the rest of the story. He was mobbed everywhere he went in Ocean City for the rest of our week there. It got to be sickening! Dad and Mom spent some of the money from the Navy check at Ocean City but most of it went into their savings account when they returned home (they were a frugal pair). B.G. was happy with all the attention he received from his rescue mission and shark destruction adventure, but he still had some resentment towards me. I had brought about the malfunction of his beloved shark and he was not about to forget it. He stayed cool until the time was right as he plotted revenge. And the right time came on our last night in Ocean City at Mack and Manco's Pizza!

This pizza shop is an institution in Ocean City still today, and we loved it back in the '60s. There were two locations on the boardwalk back then and we craved the pizza. It was a required activity every night on the boardwalk...You *had* to get at least one slice of pizza every single evening. It just was not a complete night on the boardwalk unless you had Mack and Manco's pizza. Mom and Dad gave B.G. and me some extra money and turned us loose on the boardwalk, but with B.G.'s fame and privileges we needed no money for pizza. It was free for the big hero! So we decided to really celebrate on our last night in Ocean City and split an entire pepperoni pizza. We were sitting up at the counter instead of at one of the tables because this gave us the best view of the show...Italian guys tossing pizza pies in the air. It was so cool! B.G. noticed that I was watching the show and also checking out a cute brunette beside me. This meant that I was paying minimal attention to anything else as I crammed pizza into my mouth. Revenge Time! My brother fired up a slice of pizza with a load of super-hot peppers and handed it to me with these words: "Here you go, Bro, enjoy your last night here." I ate the entire huge slice in about two bites and then reached for another. And then it slowly dawned on me that something was wrong because my mouth, tongue, throat, and nostrils were on FIRE! I started to sweat profusely as the inside of my mouth began to melt from hot peppers sent straight from the pit of hell. I could hardly speak as I gasped, "Coke…coke, please!" while B.G. replied, "What was that, Bro? I couldn't hear you. You'll have to speak up because it's pretty noisy in here." "Give me coke…NOW!" I begged. B.G. handed me the Coke and just as I reached for it he knocked it out of my hand. "I'm sooooo sorry, Brother. How clumsy of me. Looks like your coke is all over the floor." I now realized that B.G. was on a mission to destroy me and that *none* of this was accidental. I swear that his pupils turned red and his head rotated 360 degrees! I thought that he person-ally brought those peppers up from the netherworld just to tor-ment me, and the little brown-haired vixen distracting me was probably one of his minions. I was in real distress!

Mack and Manco's counter runs down one side of the place, but it also turns at the front of the restaurant and runs along the front parallel to the boardwalk. This allows patrons to walk right up on the boardwalk and order pizza so they don't even have to go inside. Lots of people do this, some to order pizza and some to just watch the show as pizzas are tossed in the air. On this particular night they saw an extra special show…at no charge! I was breathing fire after a few minutes and thought that I was going to die. My brother was watch-ing and laughing as he started sweet-talking *my* brunette! I looked around desperately for something (anything!) to drink so I could put out the inferno raging within my mouth and throat. THEN the peppers really kicked in and I went nutso! I jumped up on the counter and screamed, did a back-flip, and then did something which resembled the "Moon Walk" done years later by Michael Jackson. Everyone in the place stopped eating and talking so they could stare in disbelief at my antics up on the counter. One of the employees yelled, "Get down from there! Do you want the Health Department to close us down?" I couldn't reply, since I no longer had a tongue! The pain was excruciating and I grabbed a burly biker's Coke and downed it in one gulp. He had "spiked" it with a concealed bottle of Jack Daniels' whiskey, and I was now on fire and half-drunk! Plus the biker wanted to kill me! I continued to jump around on top of the counter as the pain intensified, and I discovered an interesting thing: whiskey will NOT help when you've consumed large amounts of super-hot hot peppers. I accidentally kicked a plateful of manicotti off the counter and stepped into the middle of a large pepperoni pizza with extra cheese and anchovies. Now a lot of people were anxious to kill me but I was moving so fast along the counter that it was impossible for anyone to grab me. The pain from the hot peppers was so intense that I was moving at "warp speed" along the counter. I was burning up so I pulled off my shirt and continued to gyrate on the counter. A couple of girls walked up from elsewhere on the boardwalk, took one look at me, and thought it was a dance contest. One of them tried to stuff a dollar bill into my shorts as I went by while the other girl yelled, "Yeah baby, take it all off!" As I continued to "strut my stuff" a trio of black kids came by to get some pizza, saw me, and started laughing hysterically. The walked away with their pizza and continued to look back at me and laugh while one exclaimed, "He's not a bad dancer…for a white boy!" (I never did make it to Baltimore's *Buddy Dean Show* or Dick Clark's *American Bandstand*.) The hot peppers continued to burn…all the way down. It was the most intense pain I've ever known, and I find it hard to believe that my brother had the audacity to laugh at me during this ordeal. He actually had people shaking his hand

and patting him on the back while they said things like: "Way to go, man, that was so cool!" and "Your brother is such a loser. He deserves this!" and "Hey man, I've got five bucks for you if you can fire up that punk one more time!" It was a tough crowd in the old pizza parlor that night, I tell you.

I finally had some old lady express sympathy for me by handing me a big glass of water. I chugged it down as fast as I could just to try to get some relief, but to no avail. The inside of my mouth was so hot that steam spewed out after I consumed the water. The peppers seemed to mount a counter-attack when I attempted to cool them down, and I felt another sudden blast of heat and pain. This was the most intense pain of the entire episode, and I reacted with two back-flips and a cartwheel back across the top of the counter. I then had what someone later described as "seizure-like convulsions" before going into another series of dance-like gyrations. This was my most bizarre set of moves because the pain was now unbear-able and I was praying for death to come quickly. I had no control of my pain-wracked body as I gyrated and writhed like a short-circuited mechanical shark doing the Macarena after being hit by a Flying Drop Kick!!!

I'm not sure if I passed out before or after the cops ar-rived, but I was in a holding cell in the juvenile section of the Ocean City jail when I woke up. Did you know that straitjack-ets are very uncomfortable? Yeah, that's right. The cops (and a lot of other people) thought that I had gone totally wacko and needed some "restraining devices" until the local on-call psychiatrist could examine me. Dad was angry, Mom was cry-ing, B.G. was laughing, and the owners of Mack and Manco's wanted to press charges and see me locked up for a long time. It was a little chaotic there at the police station. Mom tearfully said, "I smelled whiskey on his breath. My son is an alco-holic!" and then she wailed uncontrollably. Dad said, "Open that cell door and let me get my hands on him. He'll wish he was eaten by that shark the other day!" B.G. just continued to laugh and all he said (in a whisper) was, "Gotcha!" The "pizza people" wanted me charged with anything and everything: Unauthorized Use of a Counter, Malicious Destruction of a Pizza, Failure to Yield the Right-of-Way to a Waitress, and Dancing (badly) Without a License. The only thing that saved me was our lifeguard pal, Joe. He arrived, took one look at me, and shook his head before conferring with the arresting officers. The next thing I knew the cell was unlocked and the straitjacket removed (while Dad was restrained). The cops said, "OK, you're free to go. Just stay out of Mack and Manco's from now on." Joe had used his "clout" and called in some favors to get me released from hard time at the Ocean City "big house." He also got the "pizza people" to drop all charges. I quickly fell asleep when we got back to the cottage since I was exhausted. Mom and Dad stayed up talking to Joe and thanking him for his intervention. B.G. fell asleep with a smile on his face and the brunette's phone number in his wallet. The next day we drove back home to Bel Air and I didn't say a word during the entire trip.

"Unbelievable!" you say. Well, not really. It was B.G. and me, remember? Just go to Ocean City, New Jersey, and ask some of the "old-timers" about the day the shark attacked. Ask them about the night that the "crazy kid" danced on the counter at Mack and Manco's Pizza. They'll tell you it happened just like I said. And have a slice or two while you're there…for me. I'm *still* not allowed in there.

LUCIFER THE DOG

Remember Sammy back in the chapter entitled "The Revival Meeting?" Sammy was the cousin of Thelma Lou and he lived in Lynchburg, Virginia, where he attended a Baptist church pastored by Rev. Jerry Falwell. Sammy was an aspiring preacher who possessed more theological knowledge than common sense. His "revival meeting" with B.G. and me and the gang was one of the more memorable events in my life. I thought that I had seen the last of Sammy after that summer, especially after Thelma Lou told me that Sammy had moved to Possum Hollow, West Virginia (also known as Possum *Holler*). WRONG! Old Rev. Sam paid us another visit a year or two later, and it went something like this:

Sammy and his mother moved back to West Virginia ("almost Heaven") from Lynchburg after the untimely divorce of Sammy's parents. It seemed that Sammy's mother took exception to the fact that Sammy's father had a secretary at work. What I mean is…he *had* the secretary…frequently! The first clue that his wife had was when she brought lunch to her husband and found that hubbie had the secretary on his lap! Things went downhill from there, they divorced, and Sammy and "Momma" moved back to West Virginia where they had previously resided. "Momma" was from the tiny hamlet of Possum Hollow, a place so far back in the woods that they had to import sunshine (while they exported moonshine). Sammy's mother felt that she had no choice after the divorce but to return to her roots and live with her family. And she was welcomed back with open arms! ("Y'all come back now, ya' hear?") So she and Sammy went back to Possum Hollow to live with her father (Cletus, but known locally as "June Bug") and her mother (Pearl Ann, but known locally as "Big Momma").

"June Bug" was Scotch-Irish with a little bit of Cherokee mixed in. Oh, and also some Cajun. But his main ingredient was a generous helping of moonshine! He made it, he sold it, and…he drank it! Lots of it! This was no small concern to Sammy's mother. She loved her father but hated his drinking habit, especially when it was so obvious to young and impressionable little Sammy. Let's face it: "June Bug" was *not* the role model a young boy needed. But what choice did "Momma" have? Sammy's father was an adulterer and his grandfather was an alcoholic!

The solution she chose was significant. She decided that Sammy needed a positive role model to counter the negative ones, so she encouraged him to spend time with Reverend Jake down at the local church ("The 1st Church of the Apostolic Snake Handlers"). Jake was a good man and he took the boy "under his wing" but he and his church played by their own rules. There was no presbytery or General Assembly, no "Statement of Faith," or written creed. Actually, it was more of a "free-for-all" which depended on Jake's mood at the moment, as well as the emotional excesses of the people which were manifested in a variety of unusual ways. This experience changed Sammy from a mild-mannered Baptist into a foaming-at-the-mouth, swinging-from-the-chandeliers, foot-stomping, fire-breathing, serpent-strangling, demon-expelling, super-duper Preacher Boy! Sammy bought into the emotion, the energy, and the hype. He had never seen anything like the church services at Reverend Jake's place, and he quickly got hooked and never looked back. It was, for Sammy, the ultimate power trip. He was allowed to preach and had a natural ability to play on the congregation's emotions and whip them into a frenzy. But Sammy really wanted to do the "big stuff!" Oh yeah, he wanted to heal people, cast out demons, and handle poisonous snakes! He also liked to give them a good whomp on the forehead and see them fall to the floor while writhing uncontrollably (Can you say, "Power of suggestion?").

Now, to my knowledge, Sammy never really healed anyone. I don't believe that he ever cast out any demons, either. And I have my doubts about the snake handling. But what do I know? I was never at the church there in Possum Hollow. But I was in Harford County, Maryland, when Sammy returned to a less-than-receptive audience. Yeah, it was B.G. and me, Dominic, Aaron, and Thelma Lou. That was a couple of Presbyterians, one Catholic guy, one Jewish kid, and a Baptist. That's a tough crowd, I tell you! Maybe it was some kind of interfaith, ecumenical, let's all sing "Kum-Ba-Yah" group. But we weren't so accepting of some hot-shot junior evangelist with a bunch of improbable claims, especially when said evangelist was wearing a white suit, white shoes, and sideburns! It was like a junior Elvis carrying a box of snakes!

Sam came back to the Bel Air area like a man on a mission. He kept talking about holding a tent revival and preaching to big crowds. This made no sense to any of us since we had never heard of a "tent revival." We kept trying to figure out how Sam was going to get more than two people in a pup tent until Sammy yelled, "I'm talking BIG like a circus tent!" (Oh, well, please excuse us ignorant heathens.) Sammy decided that perhaps we needed a little "special touch" to enlighten our minds so he called Aaron over to stand in front of him. "Aaron of the Hebrew people, I sense that your mind is darkened by Satan." WHOMP! Sammy gave Aaron a firm tap on the forehead. "Owww! Are you crazy?" yelled Aaron, "Why did you hit me?" Sammy said, "You have felt the power! You should have fallen to the ground when touched by the power!" Aaron took a swing at Sammy but missed. "How about if I break a menorah over your head? Then we'll see who feels the power!" Aaron was not amused. No one would have mistaken this encounter for a meeting of the National Conference of Christians and Jews!

Sammy was an equal-opportunity guy when it came to insults. He just didn't know when to quit! It was not sufficient for him to antagonize the Jewish kid, Aaron. Oh no! He had to go ahead and bait the Catholic kid, Dominic, as well. Now, from what I've already told you about Dominic I'm sure it's apparent that Sammy was an absolute idiot! Dominic was *not* someone to mess with, unless you had a death wish. But Sammy was on a roll and seemed oblivious to the danger. "Dominic," he whispered, "you need to be released from the dark powers and superstitions which emanate from the Papal throne." Then in a loud voice he screamed, "I command the evil powers of darkness to release you!" WHOMP! Yeah, that's right! Sammy actually smacked Dominic on the forehead!

Everyone held their breath because they just knew that Rev. Sam had taken his last one. Thelma Lou yelled, "Sammy, are you out of your mind?" She was sure that it was time to write Sammy's obituary. B.G. said, "I'll go ahead and call for an ambulance." Aaron's comment went like this: "I may have missed when I tried to hit you, but Dominic won't!" I looked at Sammy and asked sarcastically, "Do you think that the dry cleaner can get blood out of that white suit?" Sammy just stood there with a stupid grin on his face. I don't know if he was so caught up with "the power" that he didn't realize the danger, or if he was in shock that he actually hit Dominic. We all waited for the "Italian Tornado" (Dominic's alter ego) to wreak havoc and destruction on Sammy's skinny little polyester-clad body. But then the strangest thing happened!

Dominic's head rolled back and he yelled, "I have felt the power!" Then he fell backwards on the lawn and began to quiver uncontrollably. When the tremors finally stopped Dominic just lay there staring up into the sky but saying nothing. Thelma Lou began to cry. "Sammy, what have you done to him?" she screamed. B.G. and Aaron went over to Dominic, one on each side of him, and helped him to his feet. I walked over and said, "C'mon, Dominic, quit playing around!" I had never seen him act like this before and I was really scared. Also, I had rarely seen anyone "lay a glove" on Dominic during neighborhood fights. No one, even the older kids, would dare to put a hand on Dominic unless they wanted a serious fight. His reputation for pugilistic skills was well-known throughout the area, yet here he was acting like a punch-drunk zombie after a firm forehead tap by "Preacher Boy."

Finally Dominic shook his head as if he were clearing out the cobwebs. "I tell you all that I have felt the POWER!" We just stared at him and then at each other in disbelief. B.G. spoke for everyone. "Dominic, what's the matter with you, man? You let this punk insult you and hit you…and get away with it? Snap out of it and punch his lights out!" Sammy moved back a couple of steps just in case "the power" wore off and Dominic decided to heed B.G.'s advice. "No," replied Dominic, "Rev. Sammy has the POWER and I have felt it!" Aaron just stood there shaking his head. "I never thought I would see the day that someone, especially this jerk (he pointed toward Sammy) would get away with hitting Dominic. C'mon, Dom, hit him so hard that he lands back in West Virginia!" But Dominic shook his head and said, "No, I have felt the power. I have seen the light. I am now a disciple of Rev. Sammy." Say what???

We were all amazed at this turn of events. It just didn't make sense, but then I thought I saw Dominic wink at B.G. when Sammy wasn't looking. B.G. had a sly smile on his face. Something was definitely going on, but I didn't know what it was, so I decided to just keep my mouth shut and watch. And before it was all over, I decided that this show was certainly worth the price of admission!

Dominic looked at Sammy with admiration and said, "Rev. Sam, I perceive that these pagan infidels are foolish and unbelieving heathens who are blinded by the power of Satan. They will *never* believe in you and the power unless they see a miraculous sign! Show them a sign and prove to them that you possess the POWER!" Sammy gulped. It was time to "put up or shut up" and Sam's new convert was putting the pressure on. But that's what "true believers" like Dominic should do, right? Don't they want to see "their guy" shine? Well, it looked like Rev. Sammy preferred that his new disciple be seen and not heard. After all, Dominic was forcing Sam to change the "game plan" in a manner unforeseen by the preacher boy. Things were not going according to the script, and Rev. Sam was getting somewhat flustered.

"Brother Dominic," replied Sam, "let's not be too hard on these poor souls. I'm not sure that they're ready for a sign yet." B.G. was waiting for this moment. "Oh yeah, we *are* ready! You may have brain-washed Dominic, but not me!" Then I saw B.G. wink at Dominic. Immediately Dominic roared, "Command me to strike him and I will do so, Rev. Sam!" Turning to B.G., Dominic yelled, "How dare you speak to this prophet in such a manner? You are a heathen dog who should have his tongue cut out!" Sammy jumped in between them and stated, "I greatly admire your zeal, Brother Dominic, but we don't want to resort to violence." Things were getting out of control… Sam's control, very fast. But B.G. and Dominic were on a roll. It was almost like telepathic communication as each one played his part and sucked Sammy in deeper and deeper. I tell you, these guys were good!

B.G. ran into the house and returned with a shoe box. When he popped off the lid a snake poked its head up out of the box. Thelma Lou screamed and jumped back. Aaron was adamant, "Get that thing away from me!" B.G. and Dominic exchanged winks, and Dominic solemnly stated, "If the hea-then want a sign, then the great and powerful Rev. Sam will give them a sign." Sammy's eyes were getting bigger by the minute. It seems that his bluff was being called and he was not prepared for this turn of events. Despite all of his tales of healings, exorcisms, and snake handling…Rev. Sam just didn't have the stomach for it. All he did at Reverend Jake's church was avoid the snakes (a wise move since they used rattlesnakes). Actually, Sammy was deathly afraid of snakes and the sight of this one had already caused a wet circle to appear on the front of his pants. B.G. noticed this and knew he had Rev. Sam right where he wanted him. "Show me a sign, Sammy. Pick up this rattlesnake and demonstrate your power!" I looked at the snake and whispered to B.G., "That's not a rattlesnake! That's your *garter* snake, Slither." B.G. gave me the "evil eye" and whispered, "Just keep your mouth shut and watch the show, moron!" He had hidden our dog Tramp in the bushes behind him and tied maracas to his tail. B.G. kept dropping doggie treats for him. Every time that Tramp wanted another treat he would wag his tail and the maracas would rattle. Or was it the scary "rattlesnake" in the box? (Tramp got an award for "Best Supporting Actor.")

The sound of those maracas drove Sammy nuts! He was convinced that the noise was coming from the snake, and therefore it *had* to be a poisonous rattlesnake! Thelma Lou and Aaron each took a couple of steps backward, but I stayed put. I knew that this thing was only a harmless garter snake which Dominic and B.G. were using to "mess" with Rev. Sammy's mind. They were having a really good time at Sam's expense, and old Tramp was happy to do his part as long as the treats kept falling in his direction. B.G. let Sam have it! "What's the matter, Preacher Boy? You're not afraid of this rattler, are you? I thought you handled these things all the time back in Possum Hollow! C'mon, show me the power! You're not a fake, are you?" Dominic started to laugh, but B.G. elbowed him in the ribs. No need to let Sam off the hook too soon. "Silence, infidel!" said Dominic as he struggled to suppress his laughter.

Now Sammy was quick-witted if nothing else. He realized that he was in danger of losing his audience if something didn't happen fast. He knew all along that he was afraid of snakes but never anticipated that he would have to actually encounter one during this little show with the Harford County heathens. The box he brought with him from West Virginia labeled "DANGER—Poisonous snakes!" was just for show. It was *empty*! He never thought that anyone would call his bluff. But B.G. and Dominic weren't your ordinary heathens. Growing up on the "mean streets" around Bel Air, Maryland, had hardened them into extra-ordinary reprobates! So Sammy did some fast thinking. Remember, he still thought Dominic had really come under "the Power" and was on his side. So before things got worse under B.G.'s relentless verbal assault, Rev. Sammy came up with this little gem: "Brother Dominic, I want YOU to pick up this snake to demonstrate that I have the Power and have also granted it to you!" Now that was some fast mental action on Sam's part, I tell you. The sad thing was that Sam still thought that it *was* a rattlesnake and he had no problem with his disciple, Brother Dominic, getting bitten by the thing. All that mattered to Rev. Sammy was that he "save face" and conceal his fear. If he had also passed a collection plate and asked for an offering I would have granted him honorary status as a budding televangelist (the bad kind). What a loser!

Now Sam was quick, but B.G. was quicker (that's why he was the Boy Genius, right?). Rev. Sammy was no match for the likes of my brother. B.G. was always two steps ahead of everyone else except *me* (then you're talking about *ten* steps!). B.G. never "missed a beat" but countered Sam's comment like this: "OK, Dominic. Pick up that deadly poisonous serpent, that slimy, slithery seed of Satan. Show us the Power!" Again he slyly winked at Dominic, who then pulled the snake out of the box and exclaimed, "I have the power!" Thelma Lou and Aaron jumped back (again) as did Rev. Sam. B.G. elbowed me in the ribs, signaling me to join him in chanting, "Dominic has the power. He is as great as Rev. Sammy!" Tramp wagged his tail signaling us that it was time for another treat, and this resulted in more rattlesnake sounds and more dampness on the front of Sam's white polyester pants. The young Preacher Boy couldn't stand the thought of his "disciple" becoming his rival, but he was not about to go near the snake. B.G. told Thelma Lou, "Why don't you go get Rev. Sammy a drink of water? He's getting dehydrated from dispersing all of this power!" (I didn't think that it was "power" being dispersed on the front of Sam's pants.) So Sammy, Aaron, and Thelma Lou went into the house to get a drink and B.G. huddled with Dominic. He then looked at me and said, "It's time for Round Two. Just keep your mouth shut and watch the fun. We'll have

Preacher Boy doing more than peeing in his pants before this is all over!" B.G. then called for Tramp to come out of hiding and he untied the maracas from his tail. He handed them to me and said, "Hide these before they come back, and take Slither with you." So I put the snake back in his box and took him and the maracas into the basement. When I returned, Aaron and Thelma Lou were in tears and Sammy was standing nearby with a blank look on his face. B.G. and Dominic were kneeling over Tramp. I knew that we had entered "Round Two," but I was not sure how it would all work out. No need to worry! B.G. had it all under control as he and Dominic prepared to work on Rev. Sammy some more. The poor kid! He was so over-matched it was pitiful. He really should have stayed in Possum Hollow!

Dominic said solemnly, "He was fine just a minute ago. You guys went into the house for water and Tramp came running up, fell over and just died." B.G. could barely control himself. I knew that he was trying to hold back laughter but the others (except for Dominic) thought that he was struggling to hold back tears. B.G. let out a fake wail. "Oh no, he's gone, he's gone. My sweet puppy dog is gone. Whaaaaa!" Thelma Lou and Aaron continued to cry (for real) as I sniffled and added, "He was the best dog in the whole wide world!" Sammy just stood there without saying anything. It was like watching a one-sided football game where you just know that one team is going to get slaughtered. Sammy got sucked in and never knew what hit him! Here was the "game plan" as devised by B.G. He had taught Tramp to play dead and only needed to use a subtle hand signal to get Tramp to collapse, close his eyes, and lay perfectly still for an extended period of time. Actually, Tramp was so darn lazy that I believe this was his favorite trick! He was good at it, though, and could slow his heart rate and breathing way down so that he *did* appear to be dead. (I think the dog was a Buddhist!)

Next came the zinger. B.G. (with fake tears in his eyes) turned to Sammy and wailed, "You can heal him, can't you

Rev. Sam?" Dominic joined the chorus. "Yes, the great Rev. Sammy can heal Tramp! He can raise this poor canine up and restore him! He has the POWER!" Thelma Lou and Aaron also begged Sam to do something to bring Tramp back to the land of the living. I couldn't say anything because I was on the verge of laughing and thought that I was going to pee in my pants. Sammy gulped (again) because despite all of his stories about exploits in Possum Hollow he had never done much at all there. Now his bluff was being called (again) and he had no clue as to what he should do. Remember, he (along with Aaron and Thelma Lou) was convinced that Tramp was really dead. B.G. was not about to let up. "Lay hands on this mangy, smelly, flea-bitten mongrel and bring him back to us!" Tramp took exception to these comments and let out a low growl, but B.G. calmed him before Sam heard anything. B.G. leaned over and whispered in Tramp's ear, "Work with me, will you?" Sammy didn't know what to do. He was not afraid to touch Tramp (unlike the earlier snake situation) but knew that he could do nothing for a dead dog. He would only move one step closer to being exposed as a first-rate fake. But once again Sammy relied on his quick wits. "I have drained so much of my power by granting it to Brother Dominic. I need time to recharge so that I might restore your beloved dog. Perhaps tomorrow would be a better time." B.G. went ballistic (or so it appeared) and screamed, "TOMORROW? Have you no heart, no compassion? TOMORROW? The dog needs to be healed TODAY!" I turned to Sammy and said, "Can't you see my brother's grief is overwhelming? Do something!" Then I quickly turned away because I could not suppress the laughter any longer. Dominic was also about to "lose it" and he ran over to "console" me. Both of us were now trying so hard not to laugh that we had *real* tears streaming down our cheeks. B.G. frowned because he was afraid that we were about to "blow it," as far as the ruse was concerned. He needed to distract Sam, so he began to wail, "I can't live without my dog! Life is not worth living without him!" Tramp liked this and started to wag his tail but B.G. quickly grabbed it before Sam noticed. Dominic walked back over toward Sammy and whispered, "You have to do something! He's crazy about that dog. I'm afraid he may try to hurt himself if you can't heal Tramp!" Sammy's eyes got big. "You mean suicide?" Dominic stifled a grin. "Yeah, suicide. That's it. His grief is so intense that he may try to kill himself. You have to do something!"

Now Sammy was really worried. He had a dead dog that he could not resurrect and a near-suicidal kid that he could not deter. But worst of all, Sammy was looking pretty powerless. Old Rev. Sam just didn't seem to have the power any more. Preacher Boy just didn't have the "juice" when he most needed it. Suddenly Dominic ran back over to Tramp and kneeled down beside him. He put an arm around B.G.'s shoulders and put his other arm around Tramp. He briefly turned to Sammy and said mournfully, "I can't bear to see my best friend grieve like this." Then Dominic turned back to Tramp and said, "Tramp, I command you to return to us from the netherworld. Return now to your beloved master, to Milk Bones, to chasing rabbits and peeing on fire hydrants. Return now!" B.G. gave Tramp "the signal" and the dog jumped up and wagged his tail. He gave Dominic and B.G. a bunch of slobbery doggie kisses and then came to me for a pat on the head. Next stop was Thelma Lou and Aaron who smothered the mutt with hugs and kisses. Remember, they really believed that Tramp was back from the dead. (We finally told them the truth after Sammy returned to Possum Hollow.) Sammy got all wide-eyed just before he fainted.

While Sammy was "out" Aaron and Thelma Lou continued to give Tramp all the lovin' he could take. B.G., Dominic, and I ran into the house where we collapsed because of uncontrollable laughter. Dominic and I were laughing so hard that we cried, while B.G. rolled on the floor yelling, "He fell for that! The idiot fell for that!" This went on for about ten minutes and finally B.G. said, "OK, time to pull it together guys. We still have Round Three to go. We're not done with this punk quite yet." I was absolutely thrilled to be included in the plan with my brother and Dominic since I was usually "on the outside looking in." B.G. had me check outside and report back. "He's awake but still pretty groggy," I said. B.G. looked at me and Dominic. "Just follow my lead, OK?" We nodded in agreement and off we went. I was thrilled to see someone else bear the brunt of one of my brother's schemes because I was usually the unwilling victim.

B.G. approached Sammy and asked, "Are you feeling better, Rev. Sam?" Sammy didn't look so good. "I don't believe it," he whined, "I just don't believe it!" B.G. grinned and replied, "Don't believe what? You don't believe that Brother Dominic has as much power as you? C'mon, you saw him handle that poisonous rattlesnake AND bring Tramp back from the dead. You saw it with your own two eyes! It was so amazing that you fainted!" Sammy struggled to his feet. "He only has what power I gave him! I am the one who really has the most power. He is merely my disciple!" Sammy was regaining his attitude. He was not about to be upstaged by Dominic (even though the score was: Dominic [2] and Sammy [0] at this point in the game). "Well then," said B.G. slyly, "I guess we'll just have to have another test because so far Dominic seems to be kicking your butt here in the Miracle Olympics. I mean, he handled the poisonous snake and brought Tramp back from the dead. All you did was faint and wet yourself. Maybe you accidentally slapped *yourself* in the forehead and got slain. What do you think?" Sammy's face got redder by the minute. B.G. really knew how to push Preacher Boy's buttons! My "bro" was on a roll. "It seems to me that the next event should be an exorcism, 'cause we've already done the poisonous snake thing and raising of the dead dog. What do you think there, Brother Dominic?" Dominic wasn't sure of the plan but he had faith in "the man with the plan" (B.G.). Dominic replied, "I have the power, more than Sammy, and I'm ready." B.G. turned to Sammy and grinned. "So what do you think, Rev. Sammy? Are you ready to cast out a demon and prove to us once and for all that you're numero uno, that you're *not* a big fake, and that you're better than Dominic?"

Now, if Sammy had any sense at all he would have quit at this point and just started walking back to Possum Hollow. He had seen Dominic handle what appeared to be a poisonous rattlesnake with no ill effects. He had seen Dominic apparently raise Tramp from the dead. All that Sam had done was wet his pants and faint! But his ego just wouldn't let him give up. He had a reputation to maintain! And Sammy was convinced that he had the "Power." Even though he had never done any of the things that he claimed, he was convinced that he was someone special with a special gift. His "delusions of grandeur" were the driving force in his life. So he got sucked even deeper into the vortex, into the abyss, into the warped world of B.G. where opponents were shredded. No one with any sense would accept a challenge from B.G. because no one stood a chance against him. It was like a chess match against a Grand Master. My brother was always multiple moves ahead of any opponent and loved to toy with them while he broke their will. He was determined to embarrass and humble Sammy. In the end, he planned to send Preacher Boy back to his mommy in Possum Hollow. Sammy would return with "his tail between his legs," a whining, sniffling, broken boy with urine stains on the front of his polyester pants. It was not a pretty sight to watch as B.G. took Sammy "down a few notches" but it had to be done. And B.G. was just the guy to do it!

Sammy couldn't resist the challenge and couldn't stand the thought of Dominic upstaging him. He was also tired of the insults and sneers from B.G. His head had cleared from the fainting incident and Sammy had his "second wind." So he foolishly said, "I welcome any challenge! I'll prove once and for all that I'm no fake and that I DO have the power! And I'll show you heathens that I am greater than this imposter, Dominic!" WOW! That's pretty tough talk from a wimp who fainted and wet his pants! Especially after the "imposter" apparently hugged a rattlesnake and resurrected a dead dog! Go,

Sammy! (What an idiot!) B.G. smiled and said, "Now that's what I like to hear! I admire a guy who doesn't quit. Let's go." And off we went with B.G. leading the way. No one (except Dominic) knew what he had planned as we followed him through the woods for about ten minutes. I realized that the path we were taking led to a junkyard on the other side of the woods, but I knew of no reason why we should go there. I did know one thing for certain. We typically avoided going anywhere near the junkyard. It was owned by "Old Man Johnson," a black man who did not like kids hanging around and possibly stealing car parts from the junkyard. The thefts had gotten so bad, despite a ten-foot high chain link fence with strands of barbed wire on the top, that Mr. Johnson had added a guard dog. Now Mr. Johnson was not a bad guy. He just could not afford to have people stealing from him. So he guarded the junkyard during the day in-between sales of used auto parts. He patrolled with a BB gun but none of the local kids realized that. The tales had been embellished to the point where Johnson was rumored to be carrying a 12-gauge shotgun. It was said that he would "shoot on sight" and then hang the body on the fence as a warning to others. This sounded a little far-fetched to us, but it was still a deterrent. We usually kept plenty of space between us and the junkyard fence.

This part of the story was *not* embellished: the dog! Or should I say: THE DOG!!! Mr. Johnson had finally gotten a guard dog to help with the theft problem. He adopted the dog when it was still a puppy; as a result, the dog was fiercely loyal to Johnson and very protective of him and the junkyard. Mr. Johnson usually left each evening around 6:00 PM and that's when the dog "earned his keep." That dog patrolled along the inside of the fence every night, "rain or shine," in sleet, snow, freezing temperatures…you name it! The dog circled the perimeter every few minutes, barking and growling and snarling at anything that moved. The "after-hours" thefts which typically occurred under cover of darkness after Mr. Johnson left became a thing of the past. NO ONE wanted to mess with this mutt! And with good reason! The dog was huge and probably weighed 150 pounds. It was brown and black and tan…and MEAN! It was part Doberman, part German Shepherd, part Rottweiler, and all vicious! And the dog's name was…LUCIFER! Yeah, that's right. This killing machine was named after the Prince of Darkness! This dog was so mean that the demons were probably afraid of it and voted to kick it out of hell. If you went anywhere near the fence Lucifer would come running toward you and crash into the fence, lunging, snarling, and growling. He would bite at the fence to try to get to you and his eyes would roll back in his head and turn red. He would foam at the mouth while digging at the ground in an attempt to get under the fence and attack you. He would jump up on the fence and attempt to climb it to get to you. The dog was demon-possessed, in our estimation, and the most fearsome creature we had ever seen. It ripped the doors, bumpers, hoods, and trunk lids off of old cars. The dog pulled the tires off the cars (without using a lug wrench!), separated the tires from the rims, and ATE the tires! I'm not lying! I saw it happen! Believe me, this dog was the ultimate killing machine! Cujo had a picture of this dog up on the wall inside his doghouse, because old Lucifer was Cujo's hero!

The dog certainly encouraged us to keep our distance from the junkyard. Actually, we did anyway out of fear of Mr. Johnson. We had heard the "shotgun tales" and were afraid of him, but Dad said that Mr. Johnson was actually a very nice guy. Dad bought a used distributor from Mr. Johnson one time and later took him some vegetables from our garden. Dad loved to share his produce with everyone! So he told us that Mr. Johnson was OK but we should still respect his property and not bother him. And Dad also said, "Do NOT go near that dog!" So we stayed away from the fence, the dog, and Mr. Johnson. But *not* today. B.G. somehow knew that Mr. Johnson had to leave early on this particular day. So when we arrived Mr. Johnson was gone, but Lucifer was on the alert. Yes, the "big dawg" was "in the house!" We heard the dog well before we saw him. Lucifer was barking, growling, snarling and just being his usual sweet self. I think he was upset on this day because Johnson left early and Lucifer had to start his rounds earlier. The mutt had to begin patrol sooner than he antici-pated…with no guarantee of overtime pay! Yeah, I believe the dog thought that he was in a union or something. He seemed to be in more of a foul mood than usual on this particular day. He was tossing a Volkswagen around from one side of the junk-yard to the other when we first got there. He then proceeded to gnaw on an Edsel, a Pontiac GTO, a '57 Chevy, and a Ford Fairlane 500! A squirrel ran out on a tree branch above him and Lucifer went nuts! He barked, growled, snarled, bumped the tree with his head, and did everything he could to dislodge the squirrel from the tree. He had to deal with this "trespasser" so he began to gnaw on the base of the tree (and made con-siderable progress). The tree started to lean and things did not look good for the squirrel. Then Tramp decided to bark and everything changed. Lucifer heard Tramp and stopped gnaw-ing on the tree. The squirrel was forgotten as Lucifer saw us and caught our scent. He started running toward us like he was shot out of a cannon! He let out a roar as he launched himself into the air and banged into the fence. Tramp whined and whimpered, hid behind B.G., then turned and ran for home as fast as his short little Beagle legs would carry him!

Lucifer went berserk! He growled, barked, snarled and chewed at the fence. All the while he "eye-balled" Sammy. The white suit did not exactly help Sammy blend into the sur-roundings as he tried to back away from the fence. B.G. stopped Sammy's retreat with these words, "Whoa, Preacher Boy! Meet Lucifer, your next test in the Miracle Olympics. He's certainly glad to meet you! Aren't you, Lucifer?" ROWRR! GROWL! SNARL! The dog went insane as B.G. encouraged him. "You are such a bad dog, you know that? I bet you would love to have a Preacher Boy for dinner, wouldn't you?" ROWRR! GRRRR! The dog was foaming at the mouth while trying to climb over the fence, dig under the fence, eat through the fence (you get the idea). Sammy gulped and wet himself again. I moved a couple of steps away and commented, "Those pants are really starting to stink, Sammy. What don't you perform a miracle and cure your incontinence problem?" B.G. motioned for me to be quiet and turned to Sammy. "OK, Rev. Sammy. Here's the deal. This is the biggest, meanest dog in this area and he's obviously demon-possessed. Your mission, should you decide to accept it, is to cast the demon out of this dog. If you can tame old Lucifer we'll believe that *you* are the 'top dog' in the world of miracle-workers and that you have the POWER. You can prove to us once and for all that you're the 'real deal' and that you have more power than Dominic. What do you say?" Sammy couldn't say anything since he was trembling uncontrollably and about to faint (again). B.G. wouldn't let up. "What's that, Sam? I don't think I heard you. You'll have to speak up because the dog is making so much noise." And he was. Lucifer was going insane!

Aaron and Thelma Lou climbed into a nearby tree as Lucifer bit a hole in the chain link fence. Doggie drool was flying everywhere. Lucifer growled and snarled as his eyes rolled back into his head. He jumped up on the fence and climbed to within one foot of the top before falling back down. He then started digging to try to tunnel under the fence. In a minute or two he was about two feet deep. He stopped and climbed out of the tunnel to glare at Sammy. "Boy, he really wants a piece of you, doesn't he, Sam?" Lucifer didn't even look at anyone else but just stared at Sammy while growling and snarling. "Oh yeah, he knows you've got the power and you're going to cast that old demon out of him. Free this poor beast from his tormentor, Sammy! Cast that demon out of him so he can be at peace!" B.G. just refused to let up on Sam for even one minute. Sammy was stammering and stuttering as the color drained from his face. He was obviously terrified as Lucifer made every effort to get to him. GROWL! SNARL! ROWRRRRR! Lucifer did not like Sammy one bit and was obviously intent on eating him. Dominic and B.G. stood their ground outside the fence but I decided to join Aaron and Thelma Lou in the nearby tree. Sammy had the same idea but B.G. had a firm grip on Sammy's wrist. "C'mon, Rev. Sam. Quit stalling. Get up there and exorcise the demon from this mutt. Show old Lucifer who's the boss! And show Dominic that YOU are 'the man' here!" Sammy finally spoke but only in a whisper, "Nice doggie. Good Doggie. Bad demon. Good doggie. Bad demon, come out, come out, wherever you are." Dominic started to snicker and B.G. cackled, "That's it? That's all you've got? That's the best you can do? You're kidding, right? That's supposed to chase the demon out of this mutt? You've got to do a lot better than that!" B.G. still had a firm grasp on Sammy's wrist so he dragged the unwilling victim closer to the fence. "Get up there and take charge, Rev. Sam! Show this mutt you have the power! Speak up with the voice of authority!" And then my brother pushed Sam toward the fence and Lucifer. The demon-dog took this as an aggressive act by Sam and roared again. GROWL! SNARL! ROWRRRRR! Lucifer bit into the chain link fence again and opened up a small hole that was just large enough to get his muzzle through. He snapped at Sammy's throat as Sammy fell backward, crying and screaming. B.G. let him have it. "You whine like a *girl*, Sammy! You know that?" Thelma Lou's voice called out from the tree, "I heard that! Be glad that dog is down there, Ronald, or I'd come down and beat the crap out of you and show you what a girl can do!" B.G. (Ronald) stammered, "Sorry, Thelma Lou, I didn't mean you." He may have stood his ground with Lucifer, but B.G. was afraid of Thelma Lou. She was a force to be reckoned with when angry. If she and Lucifer faced off inside the junkyard fence, I just might have put my money on Thelma Lou!

Dominic stepped forward as Sammy crawled away from the fence. Lucifer was still growling and snarling as he gnawed on the fence and tried to get to Sammy. B.G. winked at Dominic and Dominic responded, "Time for me to step up and turn on the power. Rev. Sammy just doesn't seem to have it today. You were supposed to bring your 'A-game' but looks like that didn't happen, Preacher Boy. Guess I'll have to show you how we tame the beast here in Bel Air." Sammy crawled farther away as Lucifer watched him. The dog realized that Sammy was getting out of reach and this set him off again. ROWRR! SNARL! GROWL! Lucifer ran around the perimeter of the junkyard, two complete laps, at full speed. He ripped the front bumper off of the VW and ate half of it before running over to the squirrel's tree and bumping it (at full speed) with his head. The squirrel went flying from the tree, but Lucifer paid no attention to it as the tree fell over and came to rest on top of the fence at a thirty-five-degree angle. The bottom of the tree was somewhat uprooted, but Lucifer didn't hesitate as he leaped onto the trunk. He ran up the tree to where its top rested on the barbed wire at the top of the fence. Lucifer smiled a doggie smile as he posed on the tree. I think he really had a look of victory on his face as he cocked his head back and let loose with a wolf-like howl. He knew he could jump down and land on the *outside* of the fence, giving him easy access to Sammy. Lucifer hit the ground running and headed straight for Sammy, who quickly joined Thelma Lou, Aaron, and me up in the tree. Lucifer shot past B.G. and Dominic (why didn't they run?) and crashed into the tree where I sought refuge along with the other three cowards. The tree shook violently and rocked back and forth as the four of us held on as tightly as we could. Lucifer began to gnaw on the base of this tree just as he had done on the squirrel's tree inside the fence. And why not? There was no reason for this demon-possessed dog who thought he was a lumberjack to hesitate here. Heck, if he could take down one tree…why not try another one?

Thelma Lou screamed, Sammy wailed hysterically (while wetting himself again), and Aaron and I yelled at B.G. and Dominic to "call off the dog!" (since they seemed to have no fear of Lucifer and he seemed to have no desire to eat them). Once again B.G. and Dominic winked at each other before B.G. spoke up. "All right, that's enough. Brother Dominic, cast the demon out of this ill-tempered canine and show us your POWER!" I yelled down to Dominic, "And do it fast!!!" The dog continued to gnaw on the tree and head-butt it every couple of minutes while growling and snarling and drooling. I noticed that Lucifer had his demonic gaze fixed solely on Sammy. He seemed to pay little attention to the rest of us; however, we had the misfortune of being in the same tree as Lucifer's "lunch" (Sammy). Dominic stepped forward and grabbed Lucifer by his studded collar. "Dominic...NO!!" yelled Thelma Lou. Aaron cautioned, "Are you crazy? He'll bite your hand off!" But Dominic didn't hesitate. He had a firm grip on Lucifer's collar and pulled him back from the tree. "Lucifer, down boy, get down!" B.G. glared at Dominic and elbowed him in the ribs. Dominic spoke again, "Down boy...I mean...Demon, I command you to come out of this dog at once!" Lucifer wagged his tail, turned to Dominic, and began to lick his hand. "He's tasting you before he eats you!" screamed Sammy from his perch high up in the tree. B.G. yelled up to Sammy, "Shut up, Preacher Boy! Brother Dominic has shown his power by casting the demon out of this dog. He has tamed the beast while you whined and peed on yourself...again! Dominic has the power and you have nothing! You're a fake, a fraud, a charlatan! You make me sick, you loser!" Dominic chimed in, "I have more power than you, Sammy, and I've proved it by casting out the demon. Lucifer is now calm and cool and under control." Turning to Lucifer, Dominic patted him on the head and said, "You're OK now, aren't you boy? You're such a good dog! You don't want to hurt anyone now, do you?" Lucifer looked up at Sammy in the tree and let out a long, low growl. Dominic responded, "OK, I understand that you still want to eat the kid with the urine-stained white suit. But you don't want to hurt anyone else, do you?" Lucifer stood up on his hind legs and put his huge front paws over Dominic's shoulders before giving him a big wet doggie kiss right on the mouth. "Yuck! Oh, gross!" said Thelma Lou. But Dominic just hugged Lucifer and petted on him before they fell over into the grass and started to wrestle. After a few minutes they stopped and Lucifer rolled over on his back and whined. "OK, OK, I'll rub your belly." Dominic and Lucifer appeared to be old friends as the dog lay on his back with his eyes closed. All he wanted was for Dominic to give him an old-fashioned belly rub. This was the ferocious beast that had terrified us???

"C'mon down, you guys! It's OK. He won't hurt you." Dominic's invitation was met with reservation by the tree-dwellers. "You first," said Thelma Lou and Aaron to me. B.G. and Dominic nodded so I gingerly climbed down from the tree. Lucifer paid absolutely no attention to me, so Thelma Lou and Aaron also came down. Sammy was not about to leave his perch, especially after Dominic issued this warning, "I would advise you to stay put, Preacher Boy. This dog just does not like you!" Sammy didn't argue with him but held on tightly to a tree branch while muttering under his breath, "I don't believe it. I just don't believe it!" B.G. looked at me, Thelma Lou, and Aaron and grinned. "Guess we took the Preacher Boy down a few notches, didn't we?" Then he turned to Dominic and shook his hand. "Good job, Brother Dominic! You've definitely got the power!" Then both of them collapsed on the grass in fits of laughter. Tears came to their eyes as they rolled on the ground and laughed like *they* were demon-possessed. Lucifer also seemed to think that this was funny as he rolled around with them and licked their faces. I then realized that this whole thing had been one huge setup designed to take down the high and mighty, holier-than-thou Rev. Sammy. B.G. later revealed that he and Dominic had been slipping hot dogs through the fence to Lucifer for months. They found out that the mutt loved hot dogs and would do almost anything to get one. "Music hath charms to sooth the savage beast" unless said beast was Lucifer. Then it was time to turn off the radio and break out the hot dogs because old Lucifer craved them more than anything! You charmed this mutt through his stomach! With hot dogs! He loved B.G. and Dominic because they were his main suppliers. Mr. Johnson kept Lucifer on a small ration of dry dog food to keep him "lean and mean." So the dog thought that B.G. and Dominic were his very best friends because they brought dogs to the Big Dog! Old Lucifer was just a big sweet puppy dog. (You should have heard Dominic say this in a "baby-talk" voice. It was hilarious!) Lucifer loved the "dynamic duo" and anyone with them who was obviously a friend. Before you knew it, I was also petting on Lucifer along with Aaron and Thelma Lou. The dog loved all the attention and licked everyone's face (grossing out Thelma Lou) before rolling over on his back so he could get more belly rubs. Lucifer had not been "fixed" so all his "private parts" were quite visible (and quite large) when he lay on his back. Once again Thelma Lou was "grossed out" and exclaimed, "How rude! Dog, have you no shame?" Well, that was all it took for Lucifer to ratchet up the gross-out factor. He did what all dogs do and proceeded to lick himself "down there" and then tried to give Thelma Lou another "doggie kiss." She got out of the way just in time and then gagged, "I think I'm gonna' be sick!"

Sammy had finally stopped hyperventilating and urinating. He noticed that Lucifer was now paying no attention to him. The reason: Lucifer was getting all kinds of attention from the gang and now had no desire to pursue Sammy. Lucifer was more interested in getting pats on the head, belly rubs, and…HOT DOGS!!! Yeah, B.G. and Dominic each brought one for the old puppy dog. Lucifer was one happy and contented pooch, I tell you. Sammy felt that Lucifer was sufficiently distracted to allow for an escape. So Rev. Sam, in disgrace, quietly slid down from his perch and landed softly on the ground. He began to tiptoe away unnoticed…well, *almost* unnoticed. Lucifer's keen canine senses picked up the offensive odor of urine-soaked polyester mingled with the scent of fear. He gobbled down the last bite of hot dog and leaped to his feet, knocking Aaron and Thelma Lou over in the process! Sammy heard the commotion and slowly looked backwards toward the dog. Big Mistake! Lucifer let out his loudest "roar" yet and took off after Rev. Sammy at full speed. The "Rev." was so terrified that he began to run as fast as he could, then shifted into "hyper-drive" as Lucifer got closer. I had never seen anyone run that fast in my life! Jesse Owens would have been left in the dust by Rev. Sam on that day! Sheer terror propelled him back down the path as Lucifer growled and snarled and snapped at Sam's heels. Sammy screamed and shrieked as he tried to avoid Lucifer's jaws while B.G. yelled after him, "Use the power, Rev. Sammy, use the power!" (I thought about this years later during the *Star Wars* movie craze. "Use the Force, Luke!") We all then collapsed on the ground and laughed so hard that we cried and our sides hurt. This was one of the most entertaining days of our young lives. Even Thelma Lou (Sammy's cousin) had a good laugh because she knew that Sam needed to be humbled. Actually, she was more than ready for him and "Momma" to return to Possum Hollow because they had "worn out their welcome."

So that's how Rev. Sammy left in disgrace after being humiliated by B.G. and Dominic in the "Miracle Olympics." Lucifer returned an hour later with some white polyester fabric in his jaws. Mr. Johnson had to take care of the downed tree and some small holes in the fence. All of us kids regularly went to visit Lucifer and provide him with hot dogs. And we never saw Sammy again. I guess he ran all the way back to Possum Hollow after his final (and near-fatal) encounter with Lucifer. I saw Thelma Lou at a Bel Air High School reunion a few years ago and she mentioned a postcard from Sammy. He gave up preaching and became an urologist!

WINTER WONDERLAND

Most of our late childhood and teen years were spent in Harford County, Maryland, just outside the small town of Bel Air. Two of the big wintertime activities were sledding and ice skating. B.G. and I loved wintertime! We had Christmas, New Years, time off from school due to the holidays (and snow days), and sledding and ice skating! We enjoyed sledding on the hills of our neighbor's farm and we ice skated on another neighbor's farm pond. We decided, as time went on, that we needed to be where the "action" was…in town (that also happened to be where the girls were located).

Bel Air had a small park called Bynum Run and it was named for the stream that ran along one side of the park. The main attraction was the large pond with an island in the center. This was THE place to be on winter evenings! People flocked to the pond to ice skate and socialize. It was lighted at night and the Boy Scouts usually had a huge bonfire out on the island where you could warm up from the winter chill. The back of the pond (behind the island) was the designated area for ice hockey, and you risked life and limb if you skated through that area. (Can you say "body check"? How about "no blood, no foul"? Also, there was *no* penalty box.) The park was utilized in the warmer months when people fished or had picnics (there were grilles and picnic tables). It was also (so I've heard) a popular spot after dark for couples to visit for the purpose of "parking." I'm not sure, but I seem to recall kissing some girl at Bynum Run one summer night. Despite what B.G. may tell you, she was *not* my first cousin!

My brother has visited Bel Air a number of times (usually for class reunions) over the last few decades. I've only been back a couple of times so I am not as informed as he is on the happenings in Bel Air. He has also kept in touch with more of our old classmates and this has helped him stay abreast of news there. One of the most disturbing things that he recently told me was this: ice skating is no longer allowed at Bynum Run! This is an outrage! Some of my best memories are from those cold winter nights at the park. No skating at Bynum Run? What's next: no prayer in public schools? (Oh, wait a minute. That's already happened.) I want to go back there one cold January night with a pair of ice skates and a bottle of Jack Daniels. Let's just see someone try to stop me from ice skating on Bynum Run pond! Even if the ice broke and I fell through, it's no big deal (unless I dropped the bottle of Jack Daniels). The pond is only about four feet deep! I do believe that the mayor and city council in Bel Air will hear from me on this matter!

Enough of my tirade on the injustice. Let's return to the "good old days" of the 1960s when you *could* legally skate on the Bynum Run pond (but could not possess Jack Daniels if you were underage). My brother and I became good skaters and enjoyed the time at Bynum Run, if for no other reason than the fact that it was time away from the over-protective parental units. We even got hockey sticks and a puck one Christmas and pretended to play hockey a couple of times. We had to do what the other guys did to their hockey sticks: wrap the "business end" with lots of electrical tape. I guess this was to protect the stick from cracking or something, but I found that the tape could leave a nice black mark on B.G.'s forehead whenever I did a little "high sticking" on the punk.

Now let me offer a little "aside" on the electrical tape issue. Poor Dad! He always wondered what happened to all of his black electrical tape. ("I don't know, Dad. I haven't seen it but I bet my *brother* knows where it is!") We wrapped hockey sticks and baseball bats with that stuff and Dad never had any tape when he needed it. And get this: we also wrapped broken tree limbs with it! Dad had an extensive vegetable garden and a beautiful lawn. One of the high points of the lawn was the vast assortment of shrubs and fruit trees scattered about. Do you realize that a small pear tree doesn't stand a chance against a teenager running a "post pattern" during a neighborhood football game? We broke more limbs off Dad's trees than I could count. My brother would feel so guilty that he wanted to run inside and immediately confess to Dad. WRONG! I would grab him and issue this warning: (1) "If you tell Dad we are both going to get in trouble." (2) "The football game will have to stop and all of the guys will be sent home" (resulting in a decline in our social status with the guys). (3) "I will kill you if you tell Dad." This usually resulted in B.G. making a decision to avoid confession, but he would then say to me "OK, so what do *you* plan to do about the broken tree?" I was now "on the spot" to provide a solution. My solution? Wrap that broken limb with black electrical tape. *Shiny* black electrical tape. Ain't no way that Dad is ever going to notice that! No, that doesn't stand out like a sore thumb! My rationale was that the limb was now reattached and could perhaps magically heal and be as good as new! (Did I mention that I was a consistent "D minus" student?) The final result was that Dad would, of course, notice the electrical tape and the broken limb. I would get blamed as the guilty party and punished for: (1) breaking the limb, (2) not telling Dad that I broke the limb, (3) trying to cover up the damage with electrical tape, (4) wasting electrical tape, and (5) threatening my brother with bodily harm when he wanted to tell Dad. Oh yeah, I thought about running away a lot of times, maybe to become an electrician or to work in an orchard.

Anyway, back to the story about Bynum Run. Besides hockey, we also enjoyed skating with the cute girls and frequently offered to assist those who were less-than-proficient on skates. It was a great way to get to hold hands with those lovely creatures. ("Here, let me hold on to your hand 'cause I sure don't want you to fall and get hurt!") I cannot believe that some of the girls actually fell for that! B.G. would offer to skate behind a girl with his hands on her waist, and some of the girls actually agreed. We even found that some of the girls would let us put an arm around them because it was "so cold." Oh yeah, you just gotta love Old Man Winter! Even losers like B.G. and I could get cozy with the cuties if it was cold enough.

It was the combination of ice hockey and girls that finally got us in trouble. B.G. and I managed to talk our way into a hockey game with some older guys. It was a rough game and tempers were flaring, so B.G. and I just tried to avoid getting hurt. At one point I tripped and fell, and a large and aggressive guy ("Butch") on the other team tripped over me. B.G. got tangled up with us and accidentally hit Butch in the nose with a hockey stick. Blood flowed and Butch prepared to pound both of us through the ice. The arrival of some parents was the only thing that saved us! We were urged (for our own safety) to go back to the front of the pond and "figure skate with the girls." So we made a hasty exit from the hockey game and bleeding Butch, although he continued to scream threats while being restrained by some teammates and parents. We decided that there really was no "down side" to this turn of events since we were back with the girls! So we put the hockey sticks away and offered to assist damsels in distress. And wouldn't you know that the gorgeous cheerleader I skated with was none other than the steady girlfriend of…Butch! Did I have some kind of death wish??? You can guess what happened next. Old Butch came from the back of the pond to get a nose bandage and a refill of Jack Daniels. There I was with my arm around his girlfriend, and I must remind you that earlier in the evening Butch and I had not parted on the best of terms. He went berserk! I didn't realize that I could skate that fast! I was off the ice and into the parking lot in a heartbeat, but Butch was right behind me. B.G. was no help as he told people, "Boy, that skinny kid is a real loser! Imagine anyone being dumb enough to skate with the girlfriend of an All-State linebacker!" Then B.G. went off to assist another cute girl who had fallen. I was totally on my own. Just as Butch was about to grab me and pummel me into a bloody mass of pulp, help arrived. A Harford County deputy was on patrol and stopped in to check on things there at Bynum Run. He saw the impending disaster and intervened with these words: "Now Butch, you don't want to do that. How is an arrest for assault and battery going to look on your record? Do you think Penn State or Virginia Tech want a criminal on their team?" That stopped Butch right in his tracks. He wasn't about to jeopardize a college football scholarship. Then the deputy turned to me and said, "Boy, I don't know what you did to get him this mad. My advice to you is to head on home and stay away from here for the rest of the winter." B.G. walked up at this time with our hockey sticks and said, "Let's go. Dad's here to pick us up." So I hastily headed toward Dad's car as B.G. whispered, "You're an idiot, do you know that? That guy would have killed you if the deputy hadn't shown up." We climbed into Dad's Impala and his first question was, "What did you do? I saw that deputy talking to you."

Well, I managed to come up with some ridiculous story about how the deputy wanted to recruit me for the Sheriff's Department because I was such a great kid who obviously had "a bright future in law enforcement." B.G. just rolled his eyes and moaned while Dad responded with, "Don't give me that crap! Do you think I'm an idiot?" Then he drove us home without saying anything else. I decided, for the sake of my physical well-being, that I would refrain from answering Dad's question concerning his intellectual status.

We had a lot of time off from school after that due to Christmas vacation. Yeah, that's what we called it back then. (NOT Winter Break or whatever is politically correct at the present time! And you know what? The world didn't come to an end and the ACLU didn't show up to sue the school!) Anyway, don't get me started on that! Back to the story. During the vacation B.G. and I thought about ice skating but decided that we could not risk another encounter with Butch or his pals. Dad even volunteered to drive us down to Bynum Run, but we declined his offer. B.G. said that we had to get back there somehow so we could be with the lovely ladies but avoid becoming Butch's punching bag. B.G. knew that the field next to the pond had a long hill which was ideal for sledding (the Catholic school, John Carroll High, was later built near the hill). So B.G. decided that we could go sledding next door to the pond, have fun, meet girls, and avoid Butch.

The only problem was that B.G.'s creative genius was always working overtime. He was not content to just throw the Flexible Flyer sled in the trunk of Dad's Impala and head to the slope. No, not B.G., the Winter Wonder Child. He had to come up with some super-deluxe, ultra-high tech, travel at the speed-of-light, nuclear-powered rocket sled! And he did! The kid was amazing! He took the old Flexible Flyer from the Western Auto store and combined it with a Sears & Roebuck toboggan! He added a steering wheel ("borrowed" from a junkyard which was guarded by a big mutt who loved hot dogs) and a drag chute (to slow us down if the speed became excessive). B.G. built a canopy to completely enclose the sled (to reduce wind resistance, keep passengers dry in case of a water landing [Say what?], and provide shelter from the cold) and attached a larger parachute to deploy in case of a too-rapid descent. Pontoons were added in case of (you guessed it!) a water landing. (I'm glad we didn't take this contraption down near the Chesapeake Bay.) B.G. installed a high-tech navigation system, a compass, a gyroscope, a fire extinguisher, a ham radio outfit, a porthole, a periscope, an ejection seat, a pair of large fuzzy dice and a rearview mirror to hang them on, and an eight-track tape player! Oh, and a "Magic Eight-Ball" plus McPherson strut suspension. (OK, I made that up. The suspension system, I mean. We *did* have the "Magic Eight-Ball.") If this thing had bicycle tires B.G. would have used baseball cards and clothes pins to make noise during the time we taxied to the runway. ("Hey Bro, pin my useless extra set of Mickey Mantle rookie cards to make noise when the tire spokes hit them. Those cards are worthless! I'm an Orioles fan and I hate Mantle!") Do you know what those baseball cards would be worth by now? I'd be so rich that I would not have to try writing a book about my brother just to pay the bills! Anyway, back to the rocket-sled. This baby was equipped!

Did I mention the propulsion system? Probably not! Well, the information has now been declassified so I can share it with you. Most sleds use a good run or push and then allow gravity to pull them down the hill. I always liked that system. It always seemed to work for me. Plenty of speed but still under control. Nothing high-tech about that. Nothing that would require a permit from, oh...I don't know...the Nuclear Regulatory Commission!!! Yeah, this sucker was radioactive! B.G. recommended that I put a large piece of Reynolds Wrap between me and the radioactive propulsion system immediately behind me. Nothing like a piece of aluminum foil to block those gamma rays and prevent sterilization, third degree burns, and incredibly painful radiation poisoning. B.G. was a pioneer in the field of nuclear power and the use of that power in the propulsion systems of submarines. But before the first reactor was installed in a U.S. Navy sub there had to be some testing. So my brother built a mini-reactor and installed it in the rocket-sled. Now, years later, I am living proof of that event. I am now bald. When my daughter was young she asked if I could sleep in her room since I had a better glow than her night light. I should have been offended by her comments but I felt sorry for her so I "let it slide." I felt sorry for her because the girl (my radioactive offspring) had a third eye in the middle of her forehead. Perhaps all of this could have been avoided if I had used *two* layers of aluminum foil!

Anyway, the nuclear propulsion system was the crowning touch on B.G.'s creation. I don't know where B.G. obtained the Plutonium and I really don't want to know. If I knew and I told you...well, then I'd have to kill you. Let's just say that no one ever had a "sled" quite like this one. I don't remember what B.G. told Dad or how we got this monstrosity over to the hill above Bynum Run pond. Perhaps my memory is a little fuzzy due to radiation poisoning. But I *do* remember the maiden voyage (which, by the way, was also the *last* voyage) of the super-duper, radioactive, gonad-frying rocket-sled.

It was a dark and snowy night. The temperature was only about fifteen degrees. Snowflakes were flying as we kissed the cuties goodbye and bid farewell to Dominic and the rest of the gang. Poised at the top of the hill, B.G. and I solemnly shook hands and then prepared to board the sled. We took a look at the unsuspecting masses skating under the lights down below. The time had come for us to "boldly go where no man had gone before." (Yeah, Capt. Kirk stole that phrase from us!) I climbed into the rear seat as B.G. choked the Briggs & Stratton engine and pulled the starter rope. This was the "pre-ignition" system which activated the nuclear reactor. The engine roared as B.G. settled into the front seat and yelled, "She's hot!" All I could think of as a reply was, "Are we there yet?" We began to move forward slowly and then picked up speed as the slope increased. Gravity alone would have provided *plenty* of propulsion on a hill as steep as this one but (thanks to B.G.) we *had* to have nuclear power to make us go even faster! It was a suicide mission if I ever saw one. Halfway down the hill B.G. radioed the control tower at Friendship International Airport (now known as BWI) outside of Baltimore and asked for clearance for take off! I yelled, "What do you mean by take off? I thought we were just taking a fast ride down the hill! Are you nuts?" B.G. then explained that he was under secret contract with the U.S. government and the military to test his new propulsion system on an aircraft. He had (without my knowledge) erected a ramp near the bottom of the hill which would launch us skyward and possibly into orbit! I yelled, "I want out of here now!" I found out, however, that the canopy was tightly locked to prevent any escape. I had no parachute even if I could have gotten out of the rocket sled. I screamed and became hysterical since it was obvious that death would be the only outcome of this trip. I panicked and wailed, "What should I do? I'm going to die! What should I do?" About this time B.G. shook the "Magic Eight-Ball" and handed it to me.

I believe the stupid thing said, "Ask again later," to which I replied, "You stupid piece of junk! There won't be any later!"

I looked out of the porthole and saw sparks flying past the sled. Suddenly there was a deafening BOOM as we broke the sound barrier. I screamed again and B.G. slapped me. "Shut up, you idiot! I'm trying to fly this thing and I can't concentrate with you whining like a little baby!" We were now moving at "warp speed" and approaching the ramp. "Hang on!" yelled B.G., "we're going airborne!" WHAM!!! Lots of sparks! We hit the ramp at the speed-of-light and were catapulted upward, higher and higher, but still on a course toward the pond...and hundreds of skaters. I looked out through the periscope and thought, "Boy, that full moon looks so close tonight." Well of course it looked close! At that altitude it *was* close! I screamed again and ripped the fuzzy dice off the rearview mirror. I began to smack B.G. in the back of the head with the dice while yelling, "Get me down...NOW! If I die I'm going to kill you!" (It made sense at the time but I was probably suffering from altitude sickness.) B.G. ignored me as he engaged the nuclear reactor while muttering, "We need more thrust to overcome earth's gravitational pull and achieve orbit." Say what??? What was this talk about *orbit*? Now I knew how those monkeys felt during the early space flights!

All of a sudden the reactor kicked in and my head snapped backward. BOOM! "That's what I'm talking about!" yelled B.G. triumphantly. We were really moving by this time. The noise from this second sonic boom got the attention of everyone down at the pond and they all began to look skyward. As we streaked across the winter sky someone far below uttered those magic words: "UFO!"

Yeah, that's right! We were streaking across the sky above Harford County, Maryland, at an unbelievable speed while doing incredible twists, turns, and other seemingly impossible maneuvers. No aircraft had yet been invented which could do these things at such a high rate of speed. If I had been down below and looked up and saw this thing, I, too, would probably have been convinced that it was a UFO! *The Baltimore Sun*, *The Washington Post*, *The Aegis* (our local paper)…you name it; they all had these headlines the next morning: UFO Streaks Across Night Sky Over Rural Maryland!

Meanwhile, back on board, I wasn't feeling too well. Remember all that stuff that B.G. loaded into the "sled" (radio, compass, eight-track player, etc.)? Guess what he forgot? Air Sickness Bags!!! Ain't nothing worse than having to puke but having nothing to puke into—you know what I mean? We were going so fast and making so many wild twists and turns that anyone would have been sick. This was worse than the old "Wild Mouse" roller coaster at Wildwood, New Jersey! B.G. was so excited about the apparent success of his contraption that he never even got the least bit queasy. I finally moaned, "I'm gonna be sick," to which B.G. replied, "Not in my rocket sled, you're not!" He handed me a helmet and said, "If you have to puke, do it in here!" I then asked why he had failed to give me the helmet earlier in the voyage, perhaps *before* we started moving at the speed of light. It would have been nice to put this piece of safety gear on earlier in the flight! Anyway, just as I was about to hurl, something streaked by the right side of the rocket-sled. Then I heard the roar of an engine as something went by on the other side. I forgot about my airsickness as I tried to get a glimpse of our "guests." Nothing to be alarmed about! Just a couple of JET FIGHTERS that had been scrambled from Andrews Air Force Base because we had violated restricted airspace over Edgewood Arsenal and the Aberdeen Proving Ground! Oh yeah, and now we had turned and were on a course heading that would take us straight over the White House! I saw the jet on the right waggle his wings and the pilot on the left emphatically point downward. The translation of all of this was: "You better land that thing now or we will blow your a_ _ right out of the sky, even if you are some freaky alien bent on total destruction of our planet." (You don't mess with the Air Force, my friends.)

Well, things had gotten a little tense by this time. B.G. looked at the pilot on the left and smiled just before the presentation of a rude hand gesture through the porthole. (B.G. later claimed he was only signaling for a turn but no one bought that story.) Then B.G. managed to dial up the radio frequency being used by the pilots. The transcript later presented as evidence (when the pilots were facing a court-martial and psychological evaluations) went something like this: "Foxtrot Tango niner niner has a bogey in sight. The alien inside just gave me the finger!" The control tower at Andrews Air Force Base responded: "Roger that, Foxtrot Tango niner niner. You have a green light to neutralize the bogey." The other pilot interjected: "Echo Bravo Zulu Charlie Whiskey seven zero and one-half saw the gesture from the pilot of the bogey also. Hold off on that shoot-to-kill order! That gesture may mean something entirely different on the Planet Zeton or wherever these creatures are from." The other pilot responded, "You can take that sensitive crap and stick it up your afterburner! I've got a missile with this alien's name on it! This ain't no episode of Twilight Zone, baby…it's the real thing! This ain't no drill. If you want to be sensitive, quit the Air Force and become a Social Worker!" I won't bore you with the rest of the verbal interchange between the two pilots and the tower except to say that things got pretty ugly. Comments were made about some person being a "Pinko Commie," there was trash talk about someone's momma, and…well, you get the picture.

I yelled at B.G., "They think we're aliens from outer space! They're going to shoot us down! Do something!" And here's what my brother did. The idiot turned his back to the porthole, opened it again, dropped his drawers, and "*mooned*" the fighter pilots!!! It could only have been worse if he had "I Double-Dare You To Shoot Me Down" tattooed on his butt! What a moron! I couldn't believe it! Now if this had been a cartoon we would have almost reached the point where the coyote holds up a sign pleading for help prior to a long and painful fall (while the roadrunner grins in triumph). I heard one of

116

the pilots over the radio: "The alien just mooned me! Request permission to give him a Sidewinder suppository." The other pilot (who, prior to the "mooning" was on our side) chimed in: "Missiles armed and radar locked. Waiting for a green light." The tower responded: "Go ahead and shoot that rude alien with the ugly butt out of the sky!" B.G. yelled, "Looks like I upset them a little bit. Prepare for evasive maneuvers." Then he put the rocket-sled into a tight right-hand turn and told me, "We'll have to lighten the load in here if we're going to outrun them. Start jettisoning some cargo out through the porthole." So I opened the porthole and threw out the fire extinguisher, eight-track tape player, fuzzy dice, and the Magic Eight-Ball. These items went flying out of the porthole and straight toward the two fighter jets on our tail. (I thought I saw a little gremlin riding on the outside of our rocket-sled who tried to catch the Magic Eight-Ball while clawing at our canopy. Or maybe I'm thinking of a "Twilight Zone" episode.) Only the dice made contact with one of the jets. Suddenly I heard a frantic voice on the radio. It was one of the fighter pilots: "They're firing at us with some type of deadly alien weapon that looks like fuzzy dice! Pull up! Pull up! Abort! Abort!" So the two fighter jets abruptly veered off and headed back to Andrews Air Force Base. Do you believe it? I had scared off two fighter jets *without* using a deadly alien ray gun, super lasers, or flatulence. All it took was a pair of fuzzy dice!

I was elated! "We're saved! They're gone and we didn't get shot down! We survived!" B.G. was not so excited. "We've got a problem here." I replied, "Two fighter jets intent on blowing us out of the sky are gone, but *now* we have a problem?" B.G. responded with this little gem: "We've got a reactor problem and we're losing altitude fast. Prepare for a crash landing!" Say what??? I thought for a minute and decided it was a good thing that I didn't puke in my helmet 'cause it looked like I was going to need that thing. I yelled at B.G., "What do you mean 'crash landing'? I thought this thing had a couple of parachutes to prevent crashes!" B.G. only grunted as he frantically flipped switches and pushed buttons. Meanwhile, I noticed that we were on a collision course with…Bynum Run pond! Yeah, that's right. All of our evasive maneuvers combined with rapid loss of altitude had brought us right back to where we started this little adventure. We were heading straight for the pond at a high rate of speed as frantic skaters tried to get away from the danger zone. The only people who were *not* running for cover were the guys in the Science Club. They were out on the island with flashlights sending us messages in Morse code: "We are friendly. We mean you no harm. If you don't kill us we'll give you our pocket protectors." It's no wonder that these guys could never get a date! What a bunch of losers!

Anyway, back to the drama inside the rocket-sled. I slapped B.G. in the back of the head while screaming, "Do something! I don't want to die!" B.G. growled at me, "Stop hitting me! Do you think that's going to help me figure out a solution?" Well no, I really didn't think it would help but I certainly felt better. At least I could get in a few licks on the punk before we died. I was furious with him for suckering me in again on one of his schemes. I thought we were just going on a fast sled ride to impress some girls. Nothing was ever mentioned about nuclear reactors, fighter jets, or crash landings!

B.G. pulled out a Snickers bar and started munching on it. I screamed, "A Snickers bar! What's the matter with you? This is no time to be eating! Figure out how to save us!" B.G. just ignored me. You see, my brother loved chocolate. He just had to have it and often claimed that it stimulated his brain. Our parents actually bought into this nonsense and kept a supply of candy bars just for B.G.'s exclusive use. So there we were, just Captain Chocolate and me on a collision course with the pond. Faster and faster. Down, down, down. Suddenly B.G. yelled, "That's it! I've got it!" And before I could ask, "Got what?" B.G. put the old rocket-sled into a triple barrel roll and then hit a couple of switches. WHOOSH! The sound of the parachutes opening was music to my ears. "Oh yeah, baby!" yelled

B.G. "The chocolate did it again! I just needed a little brain stimulation to figure out how to un-jam those parachutes!" Finally our speed began to decrease due to the deployment of the rear drag chute and the larger main chute. B.G. shut down the nuclear propulsion system as we slowed down and began to drift toward the pond. I could now clearly see the people cowering in the Bynum Run parking lot. Our rocket-sled was illuminated with powerful search-lights from a number of military vehicles. I saw police cars, fire trucks, an ambulance and an assortment of TV news trucks. Soldiers had a vast array of weapons pointed at us. Butch and his gang were defiantly shaking their hockey sticks at the rocket-sled while yelling, "You wanna' rumble, you slimy aliens? Let's get it on!" I later heard that someone resembling Rev. Sammy was walking around in the parking lot with a "Repent! The end of the world is near" sign. A couple of food vendors had set up on one side of the parking lot. "Ice cold beer! Hot dogs! Peanuts! Popcorn! Hot chocolate!" A young lady who shall remain nameless was also there. She had a reputation for, shall we say, loose morals and was holding up a hand-printed sign that read "Aliens are hot! I want to have your baby!" The mayor of Bel Air was there holding a key to the city and coupons for free burgers at the Harvey House, our local drive-in. The Glee Club, Bel Air High School's chorus, was gathered in the parking lot singing patriotic songs. A couple of local farmers pulled their pickup truck into the Bynum Run parking lot, jumped out, and started shooting at us with shotguns! The Bel Air High School cheerleaders were there doing "Push 'em back! Push 'em back! Push those slimy aliens WAY back!" The also did "Two Bits." You remember that one, don't you? "Two bits, four bits, six bits, a dollar. Everyone who hates slimy aliens, stand up and HOLLER!" The local dog catcher got out of his truck with a huge net in hand. He may have wanted to capture us, but at least he wasn't firing any shotguns in our direction!

We drifted down toward the pond as the parachutes slowed our descent. I couldn't believe all of the people watching us come down for a landing. Some were curious, some were angry and ready to fight, and some were terrified. One lady screamed (just before she fainted), "It's just like in 'War of the Worlds.' They're going to kill us!" We were now within range of the farmers with the shotguns and suddenly buckshot ricocheted off the side of the rocket-sled. Now *I* screamed, "They're going to kill us!" I saw a couple of Harford County deputies confiscate the shotguns and order the farmers back inside their truck. I yelled at B.G., "They still think we're aliens from outer space! We'll never get out of this alive!" B.G. slapped me a couple of times. "Get a grip, will you! You keep acting like some hysterical moron and they *will* be convinced that *you're* from another planet!" B.G. opened up the porthole as we drifted toward the island. We were still a few feet above the ice. Everyone had moved off the ice and onto the parking lot and surrounding picnic areas (except for the Science Club geeks out on the island). All eyes were on us as B.G. pulled out a bullhorn (from where I don't know) and stuck it out through the porthole. The crowd gasped and several people screamed! Suddenly every military person and law enforcement officer had his weapon aimed at us as the commanding officer yelled, "Prepare to fire! The aliens are aiming a ray gun out of that porthole!" B.G. looked back at me and muttered, "Uh oh. We may have a problem." I yelled at him, "Well, say something! Use that stupid bullhorn and tell them who we are!" So B.G. flipped the switch and turned on the bullhorn. Whoa! Big mistake! The navigational gear inside the rocket-sled created interference with the bullhorn. This resulted in a very loud squeal that sounded like something from another world. One guy with aluminum foil on his head yelled, "I can translate this! The aliens said that they will vaporize everyone unless we give them crab cakes and a case of Pabst Blue Ribbon beer!" One of the deputies grabbed the guy and growled, "Shut up, you nut job! Are you trying to create mass hysteria?" The other deputy handcuffed the guy and said, "I'm from Baltimore and I'll *die* at the hands of these aliens before I ever give up even *one* crab cake!" An older gentleman who claimed to be a WW I vet started waving a US flag and declared, "I'll die for my country, and I will shed blood to protect my Pabst Blue Ribbon! These aliens will get my beer when they pry the bottle from my cold, dead hand!" Baby, this was a tough crowd!

We continued to drift downward and then a wintry gust of wind caught us. The next thing I knew was CONTACT! Yeah, we were finally back on Planet Earth; specifically, the island in the middle of Bynum Run pond! The wind gust had blown us away from a landing on the ice to a touch down right on the island. The losers from the Science Club were ecstatic, yelling to anyone who would listen, "We will make first contact with the aliens! They have chosen *us* to be their welcoming committee!" Then these geeks began to knock on the canopy and yell, "Come on out, aliens, we mean you no harm. Meet the most intelligent beings on this planet." Oh really? If they were so intelligent then I think they would have run for cover like everyone else when the fireball that was us dropped out of the sky! Losers! How intelligent can you be when you can't even get a date? Can you be very bright when your two best friends are your pocket protector and your mechanical pencil? They continued to bang on the outside of the rocket-sled. This made an unbearable racket inside as the noise echoed over and over again. I told B.G., "I'm going to do some harm to *them* if they don't stop that banging! I want out of here, *now*!" Then the idiots outside knocked on the porthole and held up an Official Science Club Membership Application. Now I know *that* offer would surely have impressed any real aliens! I mean, why travel light-years across the galaxy to conquer some feeble earthlings and dominate the planet when you could peacefully crawl out of your spaceship and join the Science Club???

In a few minutes the Science geeks were joined by some brave souls who had traversed the ice. I looked through the porthole and saw cops, TV cameras, soldiers with guns pointed at us, a beer vendor, and the aforementioned loose young lady unbuttoning her blouse! Suddenly there was a very loud WHAM! Someone or something had hit the top of the canopy and created a small dent. "What was that?" B.G. asked. Before I could reply I heard a familiar voice from outside the rocket-sled. "C'mon out, you slimy aliens! You wanna' rumble? Let's get it on! This is the United States of America and we ain't taking no prisoners tonight!" B.G. and I looked at each other and simultaneously said, "BUTCH!" Oh yeah, it was our old friend with the hockey stick. He wanted to kill us before when we were just a couple of clumsy hockey players flirting with his girlfriend. *Now* he thought we were extra-terrestrials intent on total domination of his planet and he REALLY wanted to kill us! B.G. looked at me and asked, "Still in a hurry to exit this vehicle?"

I decided that I would sit tight for just a little while longer. Leaving the relative safety of the rocket-sled did not seem to be a prudent move right then. Butch would kill us even if we turned out *not* to be aliens. There was no telling what the military and everyone else might do! I said to B.G., "Why do they still think we're aliens? They can see us through the porthole. We're just two kids." B.G. shook his head. "Sorry about that, Bro. They actually *can't* see in. The porthole is made of a special glass. We can see out, but they can't see inside here." Well, of course. Silly me! Why should I possibly assume that B.G. had put any kind of *regular* glass in the porthole? What was I thinking? I wound up and smacked B.G. right in the back of the head as hard as I could. "OWWW! Why did you do that?" he whined. I yelled back at him, "They think we're aliens and they're ready to shoot us! They only way we can communicate with them is to open the hatch or the porthole. And when we do that, they *will* shoot us!" B.G. thought for a moment. "What if *one* of us went out through the hatch and explained all of this? The other one could wait securely inside to see if it was safe to exit." I swung again but missed. "I know where this is going," I replied. "You plan to stay in here where it's safe and sacrifice me to Butch and a bunch of trigger-happy Marines! Forget it! I'm staying right here!"

Well, it was about this time when I smelled something burning. It seems that we had drifted too close to the bonfire when we landed on the island and now the rocket-sled was on fire. This was not good since we had a mini-reactor inside the vehicle. I yelled to B.G., "We're on fire! Get me out of here!" B.G. came back with this retort, "Now wait a minute. I thought you did *not* want to get out because it was too dangerous." I growled back at him, "We're on fire, you idiot! Now it's too dangerous in here!" B.G. reminded me that *I* was the one who jettisoned the fire extinguisher and the Magic Eight-Ball. "We have nothing available to put out the fire and nothing to turn to for answers," he stated smugly. "Just get me out of here!" I screamed. B.G. gave me a sly grin and said, "OK Bro, whatever you want." Then he flipped a switch on the control panel. WHOOSH!!! Suddenly I was outside in the frigid night air, away from the fire, heading skyward and…Wait a minute! I was flying upward, AGAIN, at a high rate of speed. What was going on? Can you say "Ejection Seat?"

Yeah, that's right! My brother decided that I was going to exit the rocket-sled even if I was against the idea. One way or the other, voluntarily or involuntarily, B.G. was determined to get me out of the "alien spacecraft" and into the arms of the military, Butch, and anyone else just itching to kill an extra-terrestrial. So he hit the switch which activated my ejection seat and suddenly I was airborne…AGAIN! Now I had already decided that I had done enough flying for one evening, but that didn't matter to B.G., no sir! He had no qualms about shooting me into the air for a second time and allowing me to be the sacrifice. He figured that once the mob pummeled *me* for a while they would finally realize that I was no alien and then allow *him* to safely exit the rocket-sled. What B.G. failed to factor into the equation was the fire. As I sped upward in the ejection seat I was quickly out of harm's way and beyond the reach of the flames (but I did have some concerns about re-entry). B.G. soon realized that the fire was spreading rapidly inside the rocket-sled and he would have to exit or become a French fry. So B.G. climbed out with his helmet on, carrying every piece of gear that he could hold. He prayed that the angry mob would kill him quickly. But wait! The mob had exited the island! It seems that my ejection created a panic due to the noise and the sight of a "slimy alien" (me) rocketing skyward. This made Butch, the Marines, the geeks, and everyone else brave enough to venture onto the island quickly decide to venture *off* the island! So B.G. fearfully climbed out only to find that he was *alone* on the island. Most of the angry "welcoming committee" had retreated back onto the ice, halfway between the island and the parking lot. They cautiously eyed my ascent as they debated if I was some kind of weapon, alien escape pod, or an extra-terrestrial version of a fireworks display. When B.G. came out of the rocket-sled things really got crazy! B.G. had his helmet on and his arms full of gear (he wanted to salvage everything he could before the rocket-sled blew up). The snow was starting to fly about this time and visibility was limited. The burning "alien spacecraft" created an eerie glow on the island. And there was B.G. with his helmet on and his arms full of stuff, silhouetted in front of the glowing rocket-sled. So, considering all of those factors, I can understand why people began to scream, pray, run, and panic. B.G. tried to yell to everyone that he was *not* an alien but his voice was muffled by the helmet and the howling wind. The use of the bullhorn seemed wise, except for the fact that it still squealed due to interference from the electronic gear inside the rocket-sled. So my brother, with his helmet on and arms full of junk (plus his squealing bullhorn), appeared to be the scariest, slimiest, most menacing space monster to ever land in Harford County, Maryland!!! It was mass panic as people ran, slid, skidded and skated away as fast as they could. Even Butch threw down his hockey stick and skated at full speed back to the parking lot. The military commanders yelled at their troops to "Fall back! Retreat!" as they warily eyed the menace from another galaxy

(B.G.). Cars raced out of the Bynum Run parking lot as fast as they could go, and let's just say that there were a few collisions as drivers made some very hasty exits.

Well, I wish I could tell you that things did not get worse. I mean…I could…but that would be a lie. Here's what else happened. The rocket-sled continued to burn and this activated a safety feature that B.G. built into the thing. It was designed to eject the mini-nuclear reactor in case of fire, severe impact, etc. So suddenly (as the temperature of the burning rocket-sled reached a critical point) the reactor shot out of the sled and landed on the ice near the still-fleeing mob. More panic! "The alien is firing at us with a deadly space weapon! Run for your life!" (You get the idea.) But please, what's wrong with a little gamma radiation on a cold winter's night? Well, here's what was wrong. The reactor quickly melted a hole in the ice and then sank to the bottom of the pond, immediately raising the water temperature to a point slightly above thirty-two degrees. The sound of cracking ice was all around and those few poor souls still on the ice went berserk with fear. Things went from bad to worse in a hurry and…wait a minute! You know, I'm positive that I've left something out. Let me think. Let's see…B.G. mistaken for a slimy alien, panic by lots of people, reactor started to melt the ice, more panic…I know there was something else. Hmmm, let me think. WAIT! I know! There was one more thing that I almost forgot.

ME!!! Yeah, that's right. I had to make re-entry after my beloved brother shot me into space. After reaching maximum altitude in the ejection seat I was contacted by an old friend. His name was Mr. Gravity! He had a special reception planned in my honor back down on Planet Earth. I declined the invitation, but he insisted. Mr. Gravity can be very convincing. He always gets his way. So I headed back down toward Bynum Run pond and the eerie glow and fleeing earthlings and some stupid kid standing on the island wearing a helmet. Hmmm… that idiot looked familiar. I realized that it was my idiot brother who had no qualms about ejecting me into space and then possibly into the arms of an angry mob. I did my best to steer the ejection seat in the direction of B.G. because I was determined to hit the punk and "take him out." I tried to yell above the roar of the wind, "If I'm going down I'm taking you with me!" but I don't think he heard me. It looked as if I had a good shot at landing on him so, even with death imminent, I was elated. My last act in my young life would be to crush my over-achieving brother under a rapidly-descending ejection seat and end his reign of terror. But no…it didn't happen. B.G. had a mini-parachute built into the ejection seat and suddenly it deployed, slowing my descent and veering me off of my intended course (B.G.'s head). I got caught by a gust of wind and was blown out over the ice. Suddenly, I heard two shotgun blasts and then wind whipping through a mutilated parachute above me. The farmers were back! During all the confusion (my ejection, B.G.'s appearance, crowd panic) these two jokers had managed to retrieve their shotguns and ammo. The fact that the military and law enforcement people had scattered in fear meant *nothing* to these two guys! They were ready for World War III, or the War of the Worlds, or whatever. They reloaded as I began to once again rapidly descend. I heard some things said about slimy aliens and their mommas which I can't repeat here. There was also a strange military salute involving one finger. Before they could get off a second round of buckshot in my direction I hit the ice. The two farmers were elated! "Take that, you slimy alien!" said one. The other hoisted a bottle of Jack Daniels and replied, "Guess them old space monster boys found out how we fight down here in the USA!" He took a big drink and handed the bottle to his pal. The second farmer chugged down the rest and threw the empty bottle in my direction. "Let's go open up a big can of Bel Air Whup-Ass on that other one out on the island!" These guys weren't playing around! They were ready to put a serious hurtin' on me and my brother, kind of like the hurtin' the Bel Air Bobcats used to put on those hot-shot football teams from Calvert Hall and Poly!

Well, the farmers never made it out to me or B.G. or the island. You see, the combination of heat from the reactor (which started melting the ice) and the impact of my ejection seat hitting the ice was too much for Bynum Run pond. It was frozen solid down about ten inches…well…until B.G. and I went into action. The result of our efforts was cracked ice, a large hole in the ice, and what some might call an "early thaw." I suspect that perhaps "global warming" was already in operation. I ended up in the water and was momentarily trapped under the ice in an ejection seat with a jammed seat belt. Just when I had swallowed most of the pond water and decided that I should "go toward the light" I felt a hand on my wrist. It was B.G. to the rescue! He decided that things were bad enough already without also letting me drown. He cut the seat belt and hauled me to the surface where I coughed, gagged, and finally puked. I was sucking some serious air after that as I contemplated my near-death experience. B.G. slapped me a couple of times and yelled, "C'mon, snap out of it! You're fine, you pansy! Help me!"

The help B.G. needed was this: he wanted to pull the ejection seat out of the water and throw it on the fire. It's called "disposing of the evidence" and is a good idea when you're facing numerous felony charges and decades of jail time. So we managed to fish the ejection seat out of the deep part of the pond (five feet deep) and toss it on the fire. The snow was coming down in blizzard-like fashion by this time and visibility was almost zero. Plus the ice had broken up all over the pond and steam filled the air as the reactor continued to heat the pond water. It was impossible for anyone to see us as we cleaned up debris and watched it burn up in the fire. The only remaining evidence was the reactor which, after melting the ice, cooled and settled into the mud on the bottom of Bynum Run pond (I bet it's still there). When it was obvious that no identifying debris would survive the fire, B.G. and I quietly swam to shore (but away from the parking lot and Marines and farmers with shotguns, etc). We were both suffering from mild hypothermia as we lay in the snow on one side of the pond. "I'm freezing!" I told B.G. as my teeth chattered and my lips turned blue. He replied, "Yeah, me, too. But we've got to time this just right so no one gets suspicious." It was only a matter of minutes before B.G. saw an opportunity. A deputy and two Marines were walking toward us as the deputy yelled, "We've got to check and see if anyone ended up in the water!" One of the Marines replied, "Yeah, but what about the aliens?" B.G. knew this was our best chance to "get rescued" so he let out a loud groan. I heard the safety on a rifle click off as the other Marine yelled, "What was that?" The deputy shouted, "If that's a slimy alien you better come out with your hands or flippers or talons or whatever in plain sight! And if you have a big nasty ray gun you better put it down. And if you plan on 'mooning' us you better get ready for a bullet up your ugly alien butt!"

B.G. kicked me in the crotch and I screamed. This prompted the deputy and Marines to jump back and then aim their weapons in our direction. "Wait," groaned B.G. "Don't shoot. We're not aliens. We're just two kids. And I think my brother is hurt. Listen to him!" They heard the sound of serious pain as I rolled on the ground while holding my crotch. "Oh no!" said the deputy, "This kid is hurt real bad! Those slimy aliens are despicable! They hurt a poor innocent kid!" One of the Marines got on his radio and called for help. Suddenly I was wrapped in warm blankets and given hot chocolate as a medic examined me. The commanding officer walked up and asked if we were able to answer a few questions. B.G. jumped right in. "Yes sir! We were out on the pond when the aliens came toward us. They grabbed my brother and threw him in the pond. I fought with both of the aliens while rescuing my brother. I knew the aliens might kill me but I had to save my brother while making the world safer for mankind. I was not going to let some slimy aliens take over our planet!" Guess what? Those Marines, and deputies, and farmers, and newspaper and TV reporters…believed him!!! They actually bought this story and proclaimed B.G. a hero!

The little punk was credited with saving Bel Air, Harford County, the state of Maryland, the USA, the world…you get the picture! I couldn't believe it! He could fall into a pile of cow manure and come up smelling like a rose! He milked the situation for all it was worth, and even told the media that he battled the aliens to the death! He claimed they were so fearful of his ferocious assault that the aliens fell into the fire and were totally consumed. Since the aliens were never found (and no one knew that *we* were actually the "aliens") everyone just accepted the story as B.G. told it. The fire did burn up all the evidence and the reactor was never discovered. The pond never re-froze even though it was one of the coldest Maryland winters on record. Most of the fish died and were found floating on top of the water the following spring. Those that survived developed some unusual physical characteristics due to swimming in radioactive water. The residents of Bel Air and Harford County missed ice skating for the rest of the winter but decided that it was a small price to pay after an encounter with slimy aliens. They were just glad to be alive and free rather than under the domination of aliens from the planet Zeton. They praised their favorite native son, Ronald (B.G.), and declared him a hero. He was given a parade all the way through "downtown" Bel Air (that took about two minutes) and had numerous interviews with the media. I still have a few pictures from that time and some even show me and B.G. together with the caption, "Boy Risks His Life to Save Brother From Slimy Space Aliens." Here's what it says under the caption: "Ronald (holding medal) saved his brother (holding crotch) from certain death at the hands (flippers, talons) of two malicious space creatures. Ronald risked his own life to battle and destroy the aliens while pulling his beloved brother from the frigid and murky depths of Bynum Run pond. Ronald is a true American hero!" Butch even came by our house and told

B.G. that he could double-date with Butch and the cheerleader. B.G.'s date was the cheerleader's gorgeous younger sister!

I'm going back to Bynum Run pond one winter to ice skate. I'm also going in the summer with some scuba gear to see if I can find that reactor. I've been quiet for way too long! I'm really tired of keeping B.G.'s secret, seeing the residents of Bel Air treat him like royalty when he returns for class reunions, and watching people "suck up" to him because they still think he's the big hero. I was the co-pilot of that "space ship" and almost got killed participating in B.G.'s stupid stunt! When do *I* get a little recognition? I may end up in the penitentiary (what's the statute of limitations on the crime of impersonating a slimy space alien?) but at least I'll take B.G. down a couple of notches. If you see the little over-achiever, don't tell him I'm looking for him. I just want to sneak up behind him one day on the streets of Bel Air, smack him in the back of the head with a pair of fuzzy dice, and tell him that the Magic Eight-Ball said, "It's Judgment Day, punk!"

THE FACTS OF LIFE—Part Two

Sooner or later, every kid gets some form of "The Talk," that dreaded discussion on sex. My brother and I were not excluded from this experience. I find that, even today, my wife is still explaining things to me that I don't know or understand about this subject. She has more answers to *this* question than you can imagine: "Why not tonight?" Every time I ask that question she comes up with a very creative answer that gets me so confused I end up apologizing to her! And then I end up saying something like "Of course not tonight, dear. What was I thinking? How inconsiderate of me! Just relax on the couch while I fix you a hot cup of tea, and then I'll finish the dishes." So once again she manipulates me and gets what she wants (and I definitely *don't* get what I want!). How do women do this stuff? A better question is this: Why don't men realize that they are hopelessly overmatched and just give up?

Anyway, I have gotten side-tracked from my story (now *you're* manipulating me, aren't you?). I believe that Mom forced Dad's hand on "The Talk" after one specific incident: the commercial where the gorgeous Farrah Fawcett sensuously smeared shaving cream on the smiling face of Joe Namath, quarterback for the New York Jets, she caught B.G. and me staring at the TV screen and chanting, "I wish I was Joe!" (This bordered on treason since we were die-hard Baltimore Colts fans.) She went to Dad and told him that puberty had arrived and brought a whole bunch of out-of-control hormones along! It was time to do something, and since we were *his* sons—HE had to give us "The Talk." Dad was looking forward to this about as much as getting a root canal! He was just very uncomfortable with the entire subject and also felt inadequate to explain things and answer questions. Plus, this was quite a few years ago and the subject of sex was just not talked about that much (as opposed to today when we are drowning in it!).

Dad decided that the easiest way to handle this situation was with the use of visual aids. Poor Dad, he tried. I've now lived in Virginia since 1974, and, as we say in the south, "Bless his heart, he sure tried, he really did. Bless his heart!" Dad came up with the following items for "The Talk": Barbie, G.I. Joe, a donut, a hot dog, a balloon, some Vienna sausages, four ping-pong balls, mayonnaise, a medium egg, and an eight-penny nail. WOW! Now that's an impressive list for a talk on the facts of life! (Hey, stop the giggling! This is serious stuff!) If there was *ever* an event which would inspire abstinence, this was surely it! Some of you probably think that I'm making this up, don't you? Not so. It happened just like I'm about to tell you. If you don't believe me, then just go ask B.G. (Wait. On second thought, maybe you should not do that.)

Dad rounded us up early one Saturday morning, herded us into the kitchen and said, "No cartoons this morning, boys. We have some important stuff to talk about." It must have been, since Pops had shaved (on a Saturday) and hosed himself down with Old Spice. He was ready for some serious talk on a serious matter, but we just wanted to watch cartoons. We whined, but Dad was not about to give in. "Look, you two…" he said without blinking an eye, "…we *are* going to have this talk today because your mother…I mean, I… said so!" Then he pulled out all of the above-mentioned items and I yelled, "Hot dogs for breakfast! Way to go, Dad!" B.G. started laughing, and Dad gave him a quick whack on the back of the head. Then Dad turned to me and growled, "These items are *not* for eating. They are for demonstration purposes only. They are visual aids." I didn't know when to quit so I said, "I may demonstrate if I don't get some breakfast soon. I'm feeling weak and think my blood sugar is too low." Dad said something about "loss of blood" and also "attitude adjustment" just before he whacked *me* on the back of the head. "OK, now that I have your undivided attention, I'll continue with our talk on the 'facts of life' which is also known as the 'birds and the bees' talk." I just looked at Dad with a mixture of amusement and confusion. B.G. looked at me and laughed. "He's talking about SEX, you moron!" Dad turned crimson. "We will *NOT* use that word in this house! And keep your voice down before your mother hears you!"

I was confused, to say the least. "Dad, if we are going to talk about bees I need to be careful. I'm allergic to them, remember?" Dad just shook his head. "Son, I'm not talking about real bees. It's just a phrase. Haven't you ever heard anyone use the term 'birds and the bees' when referring to S-E-X?" (Yes, he spelled it out.) My reply: "I heard some of the guys talking about B-O-O-B-S. Does that count?" B.G. was on the floor by this time trying to suppress laughter. He was so advanced in his knowledge and reading skills by this time that he could have taught Dad a few things. He was enjoying my naiveté and found it hard to believe that I was so ignorant on matters pertaining to sex. (Excuse me, I meant s-e-x.) Dad replied, "Yes, B-O-O-B-S are part of what we are talking about, but only a *small* part." B.G. chimed in, "They're not a small part if you're talking about Dolly Parton!" WHACK! Dad nailed Mr. Know-it-All again. "Boy, you are really starting to try my patience!"

B.G. was a little fuzzy from the whack and he calmed down while waiting for the cobwebs to clear. Dad said, "OK, if everyone is under control and ready to listen, we'll continue. No breakfast or cartoons until we're done. Understood?" And you know how it goes from there. Feigned penitence alternated with selective inattention, nodding heads that seem to signal understanding, and robotic voices intoning, "Yes, Dad."

Dad said, "Let's make use of these visual aids to make things easier to comprehend. First of all we have G.I. Joe. He's a guy like the three of us, right?" (And the congregation said, "Yes, Dad.") "And then we have Barbie. Isn't she pretty?" I looked at B.G. and then we both looked at Dad. B.G. spoke first and stated emphatically that he was *not* going to play with any Barbie doll. I asked, "Dad, are you nuts? We don't want anything to do with a doll!" WHACK! (Are you starting to see a pattern here?) Dad *again* asked, "Isn't Barbie pretty?" I was not feeling so well at this point and said that *both* of the Barbies were pretty. (My head was spinning and my vision seemed to be a little off.) B.G. agreed that Barbie was most attractive. Dad continued, "YES, she's pretty and she's painted up like a harlot advertising her wares in the marketplace! Beware, my sons, BEWARE of the scarlet woman!" B.G. and I looked at each other as if to say, "What is he talking about?" Dad ranted on, "She's out to seduce G.I. Joe and every man she meets. Don't let her lure you in!" Then he took two of the ping-pong balls and put them inside Barbie's top. "This is what she'll do, boys. She's a siren, a seductress, an evil woman to be avoided." B.G. had been quiet too long. "Wow, Barbie! You have a major set of boobies! You must be Dolly's sister, Barbie Parton!" WHACK! I was totally lost and asked, "Why would Barbie want to put ping-pong balls inside her shirt?" (I swear that at this point Dad turned away and muttered under his breath, "How can this kid be so stupid?") He shook his head, sighed and stated, "I'm getting a headache."

After a brief respite, Dad returned to the task at hand. He looked at me with a mixture of anger, amusement, and disbelief. "Son, the ping-pong balls are just visual aids to represent Barbie's B-O-O-B-S. Do you understand?" I just stared at him and then replied, "Well, are you going to have a ping-pong paddle out here? I mean, what would that represent?" B.G. was in tears by now. "You have to be the dumbest kid on the planet! When girls grow up like Barbie they grow breasts!" WHACK! Dad nailed B.G. again and backed him up against the nearest wall. "Boy, we do *NOT* use that word in this house! Do you want your mother to walk in and hear you talking like that?" B.G. was genuinely scared at this point and stammered, "N…N…No sir!" Dad took a deep breath and released his grip on B.G. while talking to himself. "It will be over soon. Just be calm. Don't over-react."

Dad finally looked at us, took another deep breath, looked heavenward for inspiration, and then growled, "All right!

Let's move on. Pay attention and don't interrupt me. If you have a question just raise your hand like you do in school. OK?" We nodded in agreement. Dad picked up the donut. "Barbie doesn't just have the B-O-O-B-S up top that guys like to look at or touch. She has something down below that guys also like." B.G.'s hand shot up! "Yes, son, what is it?" B.G. had to show his knowledge of the opposite sex so he yelled, "You're talking about her vagi...UMPH!" B.G. was stopped in mid-sentence by Dad's big hand clamped firmly across his mouth. "Boy, you are starting to annoy me! I'm going to take my hand off your mouth and the *only* thing I want to hear from you is my usual reply to your comments. Now what would that be?" B.G. had that whole scared bulgy big-eye thing going on as Dad un-muzzled him. "Father, you would say to me that we do *NOT* use that word in this house." Dad patted him on the head and said, "Exactly right! Now you're starting to get the picture. Let's continue." He again picked up the donut. "Notice that the donut has a hole or opening in the center. Barbie also has an opening 'down there' that guys find interesting." I raised my hand. Dad just shook his head and said, "Now, what's the matter, boy?" I sensed his disgust and replied, "I have a question so I raised my hand like you told us to do!" Dad muttered, "I just know that I'm going to regret this. OK, son. You're right. You raised your hand like I asked you to do. So what's your question?"

I was genuinely confused by this entire discussion. It made no sense to me and I failed to grasp the symbolism. I was lost in the literal interpretation of Dad's visual aids so I asked, "Why would Barbie put a donut down into her shorts? Wouldn't that be kinda' messy? And what kind of donut would it be? I mean, there are glazed donuts, chocolate-covered donuts, jelly-filled donuts, and..." Dad cut me off as he walked over to the refrigerator and began to pound his head against the door. Wham! Wham! Wham! B.G. and I just stared at him and then at each other. We had never seen our father so upset! This talk on S-E-X was getting out of hand! Dad was starting to go N-U-T-S! My brother leaned over to me and whispered, "He's not talking about a real donut, you idiot! The donut is just a symbol, a metaphor!" I looked at him and replied, "A meta...what?" B.G. groaned and muttered, "Why do I bother? This idiot will never know enough to 'do it' anyway! And it's a good thing because the world does NOT want him to reproduce any idiot offspring!" Dad, holding his now-bleeding head, said to us in a hushed voice, "That's enough! Forget the donut for now. Let's move on before I faint from loss of blood!"

Dad opened one of the kitchen windows and took a few deep gulps of the cool morning air. He washed the blood off of his bleeding forehead and then took a long drink of water. The poor fellow was determined to finish this talk (or suffer Mom's wrath) so he decided to try again. It was time to turn our attention from Barbie and concentrate instead on G.I. Joe. Dad glared at us and said, "All right, you two! We're going to forget Barbie for a minute and talk about our old pal, G.I. Joe. He's a guy just like us, right?" We nodded in agreement. Dad continued: "Joe is a guy so (if he were real) he would have the same equipment as us, right?" I thought Dad was talking about military equipment so I replied, "Yeah, Dad, I have a canteen belt and helmet like G.I. Joe, but I don't have a gun." Dad stepped in my direction to administer another whack but stopped in mid-stride and grabbed the kitchen counter. "Whoa there. Feeling a little dizzy from banging my head on the fridge. Go ahead and give yourself a whack!" I decided I didn't need another whack so I responded with this: "I would like to withdraw my previous comment and ask the jury to disregard." Dad stared at me and said, "Don't even think about getting smart with me, boy!" B.G. leaned over and whispered, "Been watching *Perry Mason* again, haven't you?" Dad regained his balance and continued while giving me the "evil eye" every few minutes. "The 'equipment' I'm talking about is what we guys have in our pants. In this case I'll illustrate with G.I. Joe by using this Vienna sausage." B.G. just couldn't help himself. "Wow, Joe! You are packing some serious pork there! No wonder Barbie wants you so bad!"

(OK, let's pause for just a moment. It's quiz time. Fill in the blank. Ready? Here we go: At this time Dad stepped toward B.G. and gave him a _____: [1] hug, [2] glass of orange juice, or [3] WHACK in the head!!! If you answered with #3 you are correct. Go reward yourself with a donut and a can of Vienna sausages. If you gave any other answer, then you have obviously *not* been paying attention. Give yourself a whack.)

B.G. started to sniffle after getting whacked so Dad said sympathetically, "Oh, dry up! That didn't hurt! Do you want me to really give you something to cry about?" B.G. wiped the tears from his eyes and whimpered, "No sir." (What a little pansy!) Dad cleared his throat and said, "Fine! Let's move on. G.I. Joe has a *wee-wee* just like us." B.G. never knew when to quit. "It's called a peni…UMPHH!" (Hey, we've been here before, haven't we? You know the drill. Big paternal hand on Mr. Know-it-All's mouth and then the phrase: "We do *NOT* use that word in this house!") Dad continued: "As I said, Joe has a wee-wee like us. It's small now. But then along comes Barbie with her B-O-O-B-S and her donut-thing and G.I. Joe gets all excited. Next thing you know the Vienna sausage is all tingling and then it starts to grow. Now Joe has a hot dog!" And then Dad proceeded to put the hot dog (part of it, anyway) into Joe's pants, turned to us and asked, "Boys, do you understand what I'm telling you?"

B.G. chimed in again (for a kid with an I.Q. of 210 my brother could be pretty stupid at times) and said, "You mean Joe had an erect…UMPHH!" (I don't really need to go through this again, do I?) I happily yelled out, "We do *NOT* use that word in this house!" Dad gave me a whack and growled, "That's *my* line, boy!" I rubbed my sore head and turned to B.G. to ask, "What was the word you were going to say?" Dad yelled, "Hey! Pay attention! Now, where were we?" I was ready with an answer: "I think Barbie and G.I. Joe were going on a picnic, Dad. I mean, they had donuts and Vienna sausages and hot dogs. And if there was a ping-pong table nearby they could take the two ping-pong balls out of Barbie's shirt and play a game!"

B.G. fell to the floor while laughing hysterically. Dad turned red, sputtered, spun around, flung the kitchen door open, and raced outside. I watched as he rapidly walked in circles around the back yard, shaking his head and muttering to himself. A couple of times he stopped and just trembled uncontrollably. I heard him say, under his breath, "And to think that I wanted boys! Why couldn't we have daughters? Then their mother could go through this ordeal instead of me!" Mom opened one of the upstairs windows and called out to Dad, "Everything OK, dear? How's the talk going? Are you finished yet?" Dad glared up at her and yelled, "Don't make me come up there, woman!" (Boy, he was really stressed out! He must have had a death wish or temporary insanity!) Mom leaned out of the window and screamed, "What did you say? I *know* you weren't talking to *me* in that tone of voice, mister!" At this point in time Dad's sanity returned and he hastily apologized. "We're almost finished, my dear Ruth. It's going fine. Sorry about my little outburst. Want to go out to dinner tonight?"

Mom's icy stare drove Dad back into the kitchen to continue our lesson. The poor man looked like he had just left his cell on Death Row for that last long walk to "Old Sparky." I'm glad that there was no gun nearby because I definitely think that Dad would have used it on himself. The poor guy just couldn't win.

Dad sighed and glared at us, "Now look, you two. I've had just about enough from both of you. Now I've got your mother yelling at me. So shut up and listen because we *are* going to finish this little discussion!" Dad looked around at all the visual aids. "OK, now where was I?" I was eager to help and reminded Dad that we left off somewhere around the time that old Joe put a hot dog down into his pants. Dad continued,

"Yes, that's right. Joe had Barbie the harlot stop by with the donut and ping-pong balls. Next thing you know Joe's Vienna sausage had grown into a hot dog! Are you boys getting all of this?" We both decided to play it safe so we just nodded affirmatively. Dad said, "Good! That's what I like to hear! Let's move on." Dad picked up the other two ping-pong balls and put them into G.I. Joe's pants. This made no sense to me so I raised my hand with a question but Dad immediately stopped me. "Boy, *don't* you even ask me about the ping-pong balls in Joe's pants! Are you that dumb? *Surely* you can understand what the ping-pong balls represent!"

B.G. elbowed me in the ribs and said, "Hey moron! Look down inside your pajamas. What do you see?" I pulled the front of my elastic waistband out and looked down. "I see my underwear." B.G. groaned and Dad just shook his head. B.G. continued, "*Inside* your underwear, you idiot!" So I pulled out the elastic waistband of my underwear and proclaimed, "Well, I *don't* see any ping-pong balls, donuts, Vienna sausages, or hot dogs!" Dad moaned and then muttered, "I could just go jump out of an upstairs window and end this now." I didn't want dear old Dad to do that so I said, "OK, OK…I see my wee-wee and his two friends. I have a name for them!" Dad replied, "I know I'll regret this question. What is the name?" I proudly looked at Dad and B.G. and exclaimed, "*Alvin and the Chipmunks*!!!"

B.G. doubled over with laughter. Dad just stared at me. "Are you telling me that you named your 'equipment' after singing cartoon characters? Are you nuts?" B.G. was laughing so hard that he could barely breathe, let alone speak, yet he managed to produce this gem: "Hey, good one, Dad! I like that question about, 'Are you nuts?' Get it? Chipmunks? Nuts? Testi…UMPHH!" (You know the drill.) Dad slowly released his grip on B.G.'s face. "Say it, boy! I want to hear you say it!" B.G. whispered, "We don't say that word in this house." Dad grabbed him again by the face, released his grip, and then snarled, "Say it one more time for me, boy! LOUD! I like the sound of it!" B.G. was terrified and began to whine, "We do *NOT* say that word in this house! Whaaaaa!" (whimper and sniffle). Dad whispered, "That's enough crying! Do you want your mother to come down here?" B.G. nodded emphatically, "YES!" (The little whiner needed Mommy to rescue him once again.) Dad snarled, "Well, you can forget that, buddy! This is *my* party and your mother ain't invited!" Dad turned to me, but I was busy admiring my 'package' and saying things like, "Alvin, how are Theodore and Simon doing? Is everybody happy? Getting enough air in there? Everybody ready for a song?" Dad stood there staring at me with his mouth open. He whacked me on the back of the head and yelled, "What is the matter with you, boy? Are you *crazy*? Guys don't stand around and stare at their 'equipment' and they definitely don't talk to it, sing to it, or give cute little cartoon names to it! Understand?"

I was in fear for my life at this point since Dad had been handing out "whacks" like they were going out of style. Plus, the man was acting crazy! So I just nodded and said, "Y…Y… Yes sir, I understand." Dad replied, "Now that's what I want to hear! Let's move on and finish this ordeal!" Dad continued with his lecture by picking up the jar of mayonnaise. "Here's what happens next, boys. Barbie, the harlot, gets G.I. Joe all excited with her ping-pong balls and donut. Joe's little Vienna sausage grows into a big hot dog and Barbie suggests that Joe put the hot dog inside the donut. Once it's in there for a good while the mayonnaise is released from the hot dog. At this point, Mom, who was eavesdropping, yelled, "It's more like three minutes!" Dad replied, "Do you want me to do this or not?" Mom yelled back, "Who do you think you're talking to in that tone of voice, mister?" Dad was so stressed that he couldn't think straight. He put his mouth in gear before his brain was engaged and stated, "I'm talking to the person who insisted that *I* do this lecture, but now that person is interfering!" Silence! Absolute silence! Mom said nothing while the three males cowered in the kitchen, waiting for "Hurricane

Ruth" to make landfall. "Guess I showed her, didn't I?" Dad was suddenly "feeling his oats" and acting downright cocky. "Let that be a lesson to you boys as to how a man deals with a woman!" Suddenly we heard a noise out in the back yard. WHOMP! We looked out and saw Dad's suitcase on the ground. It popped open (due to being launched from a second-floor window) and Dad's clothes were all over the ground. Then his pillow hurtled downward and landed on Tramp. The dog went nuts and started attacking (and shredding) the pillow and Dad's clothes!

"Run outside and get my stuff away from that mutt!" yelled Dad. B.G. and I headed outside while Dad ran up the stairs pleading, "Honey, now please calm down. I didn't realize what I was saying! Sweetie, I'm sorry! Ruth, let me apologize!" After chasing Tramp for about ten minutes we recovered all of Dad's stuff except for the pillow (Tramp peed on it) and took it into the kitchen. Dad was waiting for us and he looked like a whipped puppy. He was pale and trembled slightly. "Everything OK, Dad?" asked B.G. as he grinned at Dad. Bad move! Dad was on him "like flies on manure" and told B.G. in no uncertain terms to "wipe that smile off your face before I do it for you!" Dad then looked at me and asked, "Anything *you* want to say, boy?" This was one of the times when the "D minus" student was smarter than Mr. Honor Roll! I just shook my head and whispered, "No sir." Dad looked at both of us and stated, "I want to correct my previous statement about how a man deals with a woman. He actually should always treat her with respect and never raise his voice to her. And if he fails to follow those rules he should apologize and then promise to take her out to dinner at the Orchard Inn *and* also Pierce's Plantation." (These were two of the nicer restaurants in the Baltimore area back in those days.) "Also, he should agree that she can cheer for the New York Yankees and the Green Bay Packers if she wants. She can say bad things about Brooks Robinson and Johnny Unitas if she wants. And she can demand a crab feast at any time."

Dad cleared his throat and solemnly stated, "We will now continue our discussion in a calm and rational manner. Now what was our last topic?" B.G. and I just stared at Dad without saying anything. We talked later and concluded that Mom must have really let him have it...and good! She was a force to be reckoned with, that was for sure!

I finally raised my hand. "Yes, my son?" I looked at B.G. and then back at Dad and replied, "We were talking about mayonnaise being released from a hot dog." Dad smiled. "Yes, that's right. Very good, my son!" (He was really starting to freak me out.) Dad continued, "Yes, the hot dog releases mayonnaise and ...what is it, my son?" I had raised my hand again since confusion had set in once more. "I don't understand this whole 'mayo from the hot dog' thing. I've never seen mayonnaise come out of a hot dog or even put on a hot dog! It's either catsup or mustard, but not mayo! And it's on the outside and not inside!" Dad's expression changed immediately. B.G. punched me in the arm and said, "He's talking about sem... UMPH!" Oh yeah, Pops was back with the death grip on Wonder Boy's throat. He snarled at B.G. "Do you think, even for one moment, that we would say *that* word in this house?" B.G. couldn't reply since he was a little low on oxygen at this point. He just shook his head from side to side while gasping, "Can't breathe!!!" Dad finally turned him loose and glared at me. "You'll just have to take my word for it, boy! If I say mayonnaise comes out of the hot dog, then that's what happens! Now let's move on!"

Before I could say anything else Dad launched into the next part of the story. I made the "T" (for "Time Out") sign with my hands and Dad abruptly stopped. B.G. had turned blue so I took a moment to give him a hearty slap on the back (yeah, I loved it!) so Brainiac could resume breathing. Child Protective Services would have called the cops and had Dad hauled off to jail for child abuse faster than you could say "Dr. Phil" or "dysfunctional family!" But CPS wasn't invited that morning so we just had to endure a little bit of "tough love."

Dad continued, "Now we have a serious problem, boys. G.I. Joe's little sausage grew into a big hot dog due to Barbie's ping-pong balls and donut. Then G.I. Joe's ping-pong balls produced mayo which got squirted from the hot dog into the donut." (B.G. said, "Ejac...UMPH!" and Dad said, "Hope you took a deep breath!") Dad, while firmly gripping my brother's face, continued. "Way down in the donut is an egg (at this point Dad raised the medium egg from the counter top and held it in front of our faces) and that egg is just waiting for a visit from some little tiny guys that look like tadpoles. There are millions of them in the mayonnaise and they can't wait to swim down deep into the donut and party with the egg. I don't have any tadpoles here so I'll illustrate with this eight-penny nail. The tadpole nails swim down, knock on the door of the egg, and say something like, 'What's a nice egg like you doing in a place like this?' but the egg won't let them in." At this point Dad stopped talking and released a thrashing B.G. from the Vulcan Death Grip.

"You're all right, boy! Why, one time when I was in the Army I had to swim the English Channel and...well, that's another story. Let's continue." B.G. was sucking air and looked pretty pale. At this point I really didn't care about swimming tadpole nails or mayo or donuts. I was just thoroughly happy to see B.G. take a few lumps! Dad continued with his lecture. "Where was I? Oh yeah, the tadpole nails want to get into the egg but the egg plays 'hard to get' while teasing the tadpole nails with comments like 'Hey sailor, looking for a good time?' or 'Think you're getting in here? Well, the yolk's on you!' Pay attention boys, that was my best joke of the day!" B.G. and I just rolled our eyes as Dad moved right along. "The egg is no match for the nail so finally one, and only one, nail gets through the shell of the egg." At this point Dad punched the eight-penny nail through the egg but exerted too much force. Egg went everywhere! "That wasn't supposed to happen, boys. The nail is just supposed to get into the egg and then a baby starts to grow in there." B.G. had regained his wind and started to laugh. I looked at Dad and said, "A baby? What are you talking about, Dad? There might be a baby *chick* growing in there, but you just killed it with that darn nail!" B.G. looked at me and shook his head. "Moron! The sperm just penetrated the egg and caused a pregnancy. A baby will arrive in nine months! Barbie got 'nailed' by G.I. Joe!" Dad lunged at B.G. but missed. "Did I hear you say the 'S-word' and the 'P-word' boy?" He lunged again but B.G. was too quick. I decided to put in my two cents. "Yeah, Dad, he said 'sperm' and I'll bet that we don't say that word in this house! And he also mentioned some girl named Nancy!"

B.G. warily eyed Dad from across the room. Mom was still upstairs but heard the commotion and called out, "Everything OK down there?" to which B.G. replied, "Noooooo!" Dad responded, "That Ronald just loves to kid around, doesn't he, dear? Don't worry, everything is just fine!" Mom then yelled back, "Well, who's Nancy?" I thought that this conversation between the first and second floor occupants (wherein yelling was allowed) was pretty cool so I volunteered the following information: "Nancy is a girl that Ron said got sperm on her egg." Dad turned three shades of crimson and glared at me. "Boy, are you insane? Why would you ever say something like *that* to your mother?" Then he lunged at me, but I quickly moved out of reach and joined B.G. on the other side of the room. We all stood frozen in our tracks when we heard Mom marching down the stairs. She looked at me with an icy gaze and asked, "Son, *what* did you just say?" I stuttered for a moment while Dad just shook his head. He then looked at me and B.G. and stated, "Maybe one of you should go upstairs and throw the rest of my stuff out of the window." Things were looking a little scary until the quick mind of B.G. went into motion. He responded to Mom, "He said our friend Nancy got a perm and some of the solution got on her leg." Mom just looked at him, shook her head, turned and walked back upstairs while saying, "Maybe I should get my hearing checked. I thought the child said…well, never mind what I thought I heard." When she was back on the second floor B.G. grinned at Dad and said, "I thought I handled that pretty well!" Dad just stared at him and then at me. "If people knew what went on here today they would give me a medal for putting up with you two! And there's not a court in the entire country that would convict me of child abuse for beating the stuffing out of you brats!" Dad then took a step towards us as B.G. and I cowered against the wall beside the refrigerator. Suddenly I glanced at the items on the counter and asked, "Dad, what about the balloon?"

Dad stopped his advance in our direction. My question seemed to jar his memory concerning the "mission of the day;" namely, to complete "The Talk" with us. He looked at the balloon and said, "Oh yeah, the balloon. That was the last and most important item. Let's finish up and then I can get your mother off my back!" He picked up the balloon and the hot dog. "If the hot dog does go into the donut you have to catch the mayonnaise before the nails get into the egg. You protect the egg by covering the hot dog with the balloon." He then proceeded (or at least he tried) to slide the balloon over the hot dog. The balloon would not open up enough for this maneuver so Pops tried brute force, ripping the balloon and breaking the hot dog in half! B.G. laughed and yelled, "Ouch!! Looks like G.I. Joe just got wounded in action!" Dad gave him the "evil eye" as I raised my hand. Dad looked like he was about to cry as he whispered, "I'll regret this, I know. What's the question?" All the while he was trying to put the two halves of the hot dog back together and wrap the torn balloon around them. I asked, "Why would you put a hot dog into a donut, smear it with mayonnaise which has nails in it, then break an egg and the hot dog and not even blow up the balloon? I mean, this is one weird ping-pong picnic party!" B.G. fell to the floor while laughing uncontrollably. He didn't need Dad to impede his breathing at this point. B.G. was laughing so hard that he had to gasp for breath. "You're an idiot, you know that?" yelled B.G. between fits of laughter. "What's your I.Q. anyway? I bet it's a negative number!" (Insert hysterical laughter.) "Did you get any of this? You moron! Boy, is Thelma Lou in for a big surprise when she marries you!"

I swung at him but missed. "I'm not going to marry Thelma Lou! Take that back!" B.G. countered with this: "It's a good thing because if you ever did figure out how to 'do it' you and Thelma Lou would end up with the dumbest and ugliest kids on the planet!" I grabbed my brother and put him in a headlock. "OWWWW!" he wailed. Dad just stood there in the kitchen watching us scuffle. He was in a daze and mumbled, "I just spent two hours on a Saturday morning and the kid didn't even understand one thing I said!" He looked at me as I tightened the headlock on my brother. Poor little B.G. had started to cry. "Mommy, help me!" he screamed. Dad yelled, "You just made me waste two hours, d _ _ _ it!"

B.G. and I stopped struggling and I released him from the headlock. We just stared at Dad in disbelief. My parents *never* used profanity! B.G. and I couldn't believe our ears! Mom came racing down the stairs screaming, "What on earth is going on down here?" B.G. took a deep breath and said, "Dad used a bad word!" This brought an immediate glare from Dad. I thought he was going to wring the little tattle-tale's neck. Mom was just getting started. "I know. I heard it all the way upstairs! What do you have to say for yourself, mister? (Notice how she always forgot Dad's name when she was mad?) How dare you use such language in front of our children!" Boy, was she mad! Dad sputtered and gave her a sheepish look. "You don't know what it's like with these two! I mean, they would make a preacher cuss!" Mom responded, "I'm not married to the preacher. I'm married to you. And you do *not* use that kind of language in my house in front of my children! Do you understand me?" She looked at B.G. and said, "Are you OK, my dear? I'm sorry your father lost his temper while trying to give you a talk on sex." B.G. and I stared at her, as did Dad. I had a bout of temporary insanity and yelled, "We do *NOT* use that word in this house!"

Mom just rolled her eyes and replied, "What word, dear? Are you talking about the word 'sex' from Dad's talk?" Dumbfounded, Dad's mouth dropped open as he stared at Mom. "I don't believe this! I just do not believe what I'm hearing! You are actually going to use *that* word in front of these boys?" B.G. joined in. "Wait a minute! I've been getting whacked in the head for the last two hours for saying words that I'm not supposed to say because you might hear them. And now, Mom, *you* go ahead and use one of those words? I am really confused…and I have a bad headache!" Mom laughed and shook her head. "You have to know the correct terms, son! Are you going to go through the rest of your life talking about your 'wee-wee' like you're a little child?" B.G. was starting to get angry. "Oh, I don't know, Mom!" (You could feel the sarcasm in his voice.) "Why don't we ask DAD what to call it! What do *you* say, Dad?" B.G. glared at Dad while moving a step closer to Mom. The big Paternal Unit glared back (yeah, he was "busted") while he shifted nervously from one foot to the other. Dad sputtered, stuttered, and then pointed at me. It was scapegoat time. "Well, *this* one doesn't understand one thing that I said today! He just doesn't get it, no matter what word or term you use!" Mom turned to look at me, as did B.G. and Dad. Mom asked, "Is that true, son?"

Well, I didn't reply because I didn't hear the question. I had quickly tired of all the arguing and decided to amuse myself by singing, "You ain't nothin' but a hot dog!" in my best Elvis impersonation voice. Did I mention that I was holding the elastic waistband of my pajamas and singing to my "wee-wee?" I then did some Beach Boys music. "She'll have fun, fun, fun 'til her Daddy takes her donut away!" I also threw in a little bit of Aretha Franklin (yeah baby, the Queen of Soul) by singing, "R-E-S-P-E-C-T, don't squirt mayonnaise on me!" I once again consulted with my package, my equipment, my friends, "Alvin and the Chipmunks," to inquire if they liked my songs. Suddenly I realized that no one else was talking. The arguing had ended and the kitchen was strangely quiet.

I turned around and saw the blank looks on the faces of my parents. My brother just stood there grinning. Mom cleared her throat, wiped a tear from her eye, and said softly, "Son, are you OK?" Dad slammed his big hand down on the counter and yelled, "NO, he's not OK! He sings to his 'wee-wee' and calls it 'Alvin and the Chipmunks.' He named his 'equipment' after cartoon characters! The kid is retarded, I tell you! There is something seriously wrong with the boy!"

Mom glared at Dad. "Did you just use the term 'wee-wee' or did I not hear you correctly? Is it any wonder that the boy is confused when his father says 'wee-wee' while discussing male anatomy? What is wrong with *you*?" Mom then turned to me and whispered, "I still love you, darling, even if you are weird and sing to your private parts." I replied, "Thanks, Mom, but I think G.I. Joe is now a sergeant." Mom looked at Dad and sighed. Dad responded, "Do you see what I mean? The kid is nutso! Is he mine? Did we adopt him? His brother has an IQ of 210! Yes, 210! But I bet this one couldn't hit triple digits on an IQ test if they gave him ninety-nine points at the start just for writing his name!"

B.G. thought that this last statement from Dad was hilarious. He also figured that it justified what he (B.G.) had been saying about my limited mental abilities. He smiled at Dad and stated, "I agree, Dad. You did an outstanding job explaining the 'facts of life' to us today. I certainly appreciate your effort and I'm willing to forgive you for whacking me numerous times. I'm also going to forget that whole smothering thing. I know that you were under a lot of stress since my older brother, El Stupido, wasted two hours of your precious time since he was incapable of grasping even the basics of your fine presentation." Dad actually fell for this butt-kissing routine by B.G. and patted him on the head while saying, "Why, thank you, son! Run along now and watch some cartoons." B.G. headed into the living room and turned on the TV, but not before he picked up the phone and called Thelma Lou. This is what I overheard: "Hi, Thelma Lou. I just wanted to call and remind you that my brother still loves you and wants to marry you! And he can't wait to be the father of your children! Make sure you ask him about our discussion with Dad this morning! Oh, one more thing. Don't forget to ask him about Alvin and the Chipmunks!"

Dad and Mom also heard him but did nothing. I couldn't believe it! Dad decided to make his move. "I need to get started on the lawn. I'll never finish the mowing if I wait any longer!" He looked at Mom with pleading eyes and she responded, "I guess you're done here." ZIP! Dad was out the door at the speed of light! I swear that I heard him yell something like, "Free at last! It's over and I have survived!"

Mom and I were alone in the kitchen. She looked at me, sighed, and wiped away another tear. "What are we going to do with you, young man?" I just shrugged my shoulders and replied, "How about fixing me some breakfast? It's been a long morning and I am really hungry!" Mom just smiled and shook her head. "That wasn't exactly what I meant. But I guess you've had enough lectures for today. What do you want for breakfast?" I looked at the items on the counter and picked up the donut. I crammed it into my mouth and stated, "I'll start with this!" Mom looked at the assortment of food products from Dad's presentation, laughed, and asked, "Exactly *what* was your father doing with all of this stuff?" I grabbed two Vienna sausages and swallowed them whole as I reached for the hot dog. I turned to Mom and replied, "Mom, you just wouldn't believe it. I mean, it was the craziest thing I ever heard." Then I proceeded to give her the play-by-play, starting with Barbie and G.I. Joe. I went through all of the food items and explained my confusion. Mom started laughing about the time that I got to the ping-pong ball part of the story. She was rolling on the floor and laughing so hard that she cried by the time I got to the part about the tadpole nails and the balloon. She finally regained her composure, wiped her eyes, and got up from the floor. "You poor child! No wonder you were confused!" Then she looked at the broken egg, nail, and torn balloon and began another round of uncontrollable laughter. She staggered out of the room, laughing and gasping for breath. She stopped halfway through the living room, turned and came back into the kitchen. Struggling to suppress her laughter, she looked straight at me and said, "Promise me one thing, son!" I nodded affirmatively. Mom continued, "No more talking or singing to your 'package,' as your father calls it. No more 'Alvin and the Chipmunks' and no more 'wee-wee.' Understand?" I grabbed another Vienna sausage, smiled, and replied, "Yes, ma'am."

Mom left the room and I continued to finish off the visual aids. I heard the front doorbell ring and B.G. yelled, "I got it!" He opened the front door and I heard someone enter and then speak in whispers with B.G. just before the laughter started. Suddenly the visitor left the living room and entered the kitchen. It was Thelma Lou! Between fits of laughter she whispered to me, "We *really* need to talk!" B.G. entered the kitchen with a big grin on his face. Looking at me, he yelled, "Hey, G.I. Joe! Your pal Barbie is here and wants to have a picnic!" I threw the last Vienna sausage at him and connected with a head-shot. B.G. picked the pork missile up off the floor...and *ate* it! Thelma Lou linked arms with me and escorted me out the back door. We sat at the picnic table for thirty minutes while Thelma Lou patiently explained everything to me (without visual aids!). I learned more during those thirty minutes than I really ever wanted to know about s-e-x. I was amazed that Thelma Lou knew so much about the subject and even more amazed that she was so patient. No laughing or ridicule, no yelling, and no grocery products. She just calmly explained things to me in a matter-of-fact approach. And just in case you're wondering...it was just talking! No "show and tell" or experimentation (no matter what B.G. may say).

Well, the years went by and Thelma Lou and I went our separate ways. We never "did it" or got married. I was forever in her debt for explaining things to me. That knowledge certainly helped later on when I met a woman in college and married her two years later. I guess I figured things out since we managed to have two children. I was fully prepared years later when the time for "The Talk" with the kids arrived. So on that special morning I pulled out some grocery items and …ate breakfast! Yeah, that's right! I was *excused* from giving "The Talk" since the two children were…GIRLS! My wife insisted that she do "The Talk" since she was a woman and (let me quote) "Our daughters need to hear this from their mother." So after breakfast and eighteen holes of golf, I returned home and the job was done!

So B.G., now what do you have to say?

TRUTH IS STRANGER THAN FICTION

Every story contains some elements of truth, and this book is no exception. My brother, Ron (B.G.), has always been a brilliant guy. He really was promoted into the second grade after only five weeks in first grade, and from that point on we were in the same grade throughout our school years. He was an outstanding student and voted "Best Personality" in our senior year at Bel Air High School. He had the lead role in the senior play and was well-known and well-liked by just about everyone. I was, to some extent, "in his shadow" during our school years, but I had my own interests and circle of friends.

I emerged from Ron's shadow during my junior and senior years due to my participation with the varsity track team. I did the triple jump and high jump on a great team that won the Maryland state AA track and field championship in 1967 and 1968. I broke the school and bi-county high jump records in 1968. Those were two moments of triumph for me and Ron was my biggest fan. He was very proud of me and very supportive, and I never detected any jealousy. I broke the school high jump record that had stood for thirty-two years (since 1936) in a meet against Annapolis High School.

When the announcement was made over the school P.A. system the next day, it was a bitter pill for me to swallow. The kid doing the announcements mentioned the victory by the track team and the new high jump record, but stated that RON Hancock set the record! My greatest accomplishment was credited to my brother!

That's a *true* story!